"You're Hurting Me!"

Breathing heavily, his chest heaving, he loosened his grip a little. Backing away, Della saw the silver chain around his neck. Three silver skulls hung from the chain. "Oh!" They were so ugly, so realistic, so evil looking.

He stared into her eyes. He seemed to be trying to read her thoughts.

"What do you want?" she asked.

He didn't reply. He didn't move or blink. His silence was scarier than when he talked to her.

She suddenly remembered the ZAP gun. She had shoved it into her back jeans pocket. She reached for it now, felt the barrel first, then grabbed the handle. She jerked her arm back, raised the gun, and fired.

A spray of yellow paint shot onto his forehead.

He sputtered, surprised, then cried out angrily, and let go of her to wipe his forehead.

She took off, racing, stumbling, flying along the ground. Where was she going? She didn't know. She didn't care. She only knew she would do *anything* to escape. . . .

Books by R. L. Stine

Available from ARCHWAY Paperbacks

FEAR STREET

R·L·STINE

The Overnight

AN ARCHWAY PAPERBACK
Published by POCKET BOOKS
New York   London   Toronto   Sydney   Tokyo   Singapore

AN ARCHWAY PAPERBACK *Original*

An Archway Paperback published by
POCKET BOOKS, a division of Simon & Schuster Inc.
1230 Avenue of the Americas, New York, NY 10020

ISBN: 0-671-74650-2

First Archway Paperback printing October 1989

15 14 13 12

AN ARCHWAY PAPERBACK and colophon are
registered trademarks of Simon & Schuster Inc.

Printed in the U.S.A.

IL 6+

chapter

1

Della O'Connor tugged the combination lock, wondering why she could never get it to open on the first try. All the way down the long hall, locker doors slammed and kids laughed and shouted to each other, the daily celebration of school letting out.

The lock pulled open on the third try. She removed it and swung open the locker door, groaning as the heart on the inside of the door came into view. Last September someone had scratched the heart, and the words DELLA & GARY inside it, into the gray paint.

For the hundredth time Della told herself to find something to cover it up. She didn't want to be reminded of Gary every time she opened her locker.

She had angrily broken up with him three weeks ago, never dreaming that he would take her seriously, that they wouldn't make up in time for the spring prom. But the prom had come and gone— and Gary was just gone! He hadn't called her since their fight. And whenever she ran into him in the halls at school, he passed right by without giving her a chance to say anything.

Della was looking forward to the Outdoors Club overnight. Gary would be there, and she would be able to apologize to him then. She pictured him smiling at her. Staring at the heart on the locker door, she pictured his wavy blond hair, his lively brown eyes, the way they crinkled when he smiled at her, the tiny freckles on his cheeks. The overnight will be so romantic, she thought. Camping out all night under the stars. Just the two of us . . .

Of course, the other members of the Outdoors Club would be there too—including Suki Thomas, who had obviously joined just to be close to Gary. But Della wasn't worried about Suki. She was confident she could get Gary back if she could talk with him. Well . . . fairly confident.

She tossed her books to the floor of the locker and fixed her hair, peering into the small, square mirror she had attached to the locker door above the heart. With her pale skin, her bright, green eyes, her long, straight black hair, Della was very pretty. She was thin, with a model's figure. She always looked calm, cool, and together, even when she didn't feel that way.

Slamming the locker shut, she was surprised to see her friend Maia Franklin standing beside her. "Maia—how long have you been standing there?"

"Not long. How do you get your hair to do that?" Maia asked.

"Do what?"

"Be straight."

They both laughed. Maia had short, auburn hair,

2

the curliest hair anyone had ever seen, probably curly enough to make the *Guinness Book of World Records!* With her round eyeglasses and her short, boyish figure, she reminded Della of Orphan Annie.

"Are you going to the Outdoors Club meeting?" Maia asked.

"Of course." Della jammed the combination lock shut. "Hey—did your parents give you permission to go on the overnight?"

"Yeah. Finally. After calling Mr. Abner five times and making him reassure them that it was going to be properly chaperoned and making him promise he'd keep his eye especially on me at all times."

Maia's parents were so strict with her. They treated her like a ten-year-old. "What's their problem, anyway?" Della asked, shaking her head.

"I don't know. I guess they think if I spend the night camping out on an island where there are boys, I'm going to behave like a rabbit in heat."

"And what's wrong with that?" Della asked.

Both girls entered Mr. Abner's classroom laughing. Three other members of the Outdoors Club were already there, sitting together in the front row. Gary was talking to Suki Thomas. He looked up for a split second, and when he saw that it was Della, he quickly turned his attention back to Suki.

Suki seemed very pleased to have his attention. She was smiling at him and resting a hand on his arm. At first glance, Suki seemed an unlikely candidate for the Outdoors Club. She was very punky looking, with spiky platinum hair and four earrings in each ear. She was wearing a tight black sweater with a long, deliberate tear in one sleeve, and a very short black leather skirt over dark purple tights. The purple of the tights matched her lipstick perfectly.

Look at Gary making goo-goo eyes at Suki, pretending he doesn't see me, Della told herself. What do boys see in her anyway? She didn't have to ask that question. Everyone in school knew the answer. Suki had quite a reputation.

Pete Goodwin said hi and flashed Della a smile as she and Maia headed to join everyone in the front row. He's kind of good-looking, Della thought, sitting down next to him, even though he's so straight. Pete had short brown hair and serious, brown eyes. He was very preppy looking. Some of his friends even called him "The Prep," which he didn't seem to mind.

"Where's Abner?" Della asked him, lowering herself into the seat, resting her arms on the flip-down desk. She watched Suki patting Gary's arm.

"He was called to the office, said he'd be right back," Pete said. "How's it going, Della?"

"Fine, I guess."

The windows were open. A soft spring breeze floated in. The sweet smell of fresh-cut grass blew into the room. Della could hear the *thwack thwack* of tennis balls being hit from the tennis courts beyond the teachers' parking lot.

"Guess we'll be planning the overnight today," Pete said awkwardly.

"Guess so," Della replied just as awkwardly.

Della cleared her throat loudly and scooted her chair forward, trying to get Gary's attention. But he refused to turn around, keeping his gaze firmly fixed on Suki, who was pulling at the threads of his sweater sleeve as she talked to him.

"Uh-oh. Look what just climbed out from behind his rock," Maia warned Della in a loud whisper.

Everyone looked up as Ricky Schorr bounced into the room. Ricky was wearing an oversized white T-shirt with big black letters across the front that read: NOTHING TO SAY. This pretty much summed up Ricky's sense of humor, in the opinion of most Shadyside High students. Ricky tried so hard to be funny all the time, and the fact that he tried so hard was the only funny thing about him.

He was short and chubby. His clothes always seemed to be a size or two too big for him, and his black hair, which was never combed, fell down in tangles over his forehead. He was always pushing it back with a pudgy hand.

Walking quickly, Ricky headed to the front of the room. "Don't applaud. Just throw money," he said, and laughed an exaggeratedly loud laugh.

The other five members of the Outdoors Club groaned in unison. It was a response Ricky was accustomed to. The smile didn't drop from his face.

"Okay. Quiz time," he announced. "Take out a sheet of paper and number from one to two thousand. No—only kidding," he added quickly. "Here. Take a look at this." He held up a sprig of leaves, which he dropped onto Gary's desk.

"What's this supposed to be?" Gary asked, looking away from Suki for the first time.

"This is the Outdoors Club, right?" Ricky asked, grinning. He pointed at the leaves on Gary's desk. "Identify those. I bet you can't."

5

Gary looked confused. He picked up the leaves. "You want me to identify these?"

"Yeah. You're the club president. Identify them."

Gary held the leaves up close to his face and turned them over and over in his hands, studying them.

"Come on, Gary. You can do it," Pete urged.

"No, he can't," Ricky said, leaning over Gary's desk.

"Uh . . . it's from some kind of tree, right?" Gary asked. "Beech tree? Sassafras?"

Ricky shook his head, very pleased with himself.

Gary hated to be wrong. He slapped the narrow leaves against his hand. "Aw, who cares?" he said grumpily.

"You *should* care," Ricky told him. "It's poison ivy!" He burst out laughing.

"Huh?" Gary angrily jumped up from the chair, the leaves still gripped tightly in his hand. Ricky tried to get away, but Gary was too fast for him. He wrestled Ricky down to the floor and started rubbing the leaves on Ricky's face and forehead.

Ricky was laughing and screaming at the same time, struggling helplessly to get away. Della, Suki, Pete, and Maia were loudly cheering Gary on.

"What's going on here?" a voice called loudly from the doorway.

Everyone turned to see Mr. Abner stride into the room, his long legs bringing him quickly to the scene of the wrestling match. "Gary, get off him. What are you doing?"

Gary, breathing heavily, backed away. "Just getting ready for the overnight," he told the tall, lanky teacher. "We're having a little poison-ivy identification here."

Ricky groaned, rolled over, and slowly struggled to his feet. His T-shirt had rolled up and a wide expanse of white belly protruded.

"Poison ivy?" Mr. Abner looked confused. He reached out and took the leaves from Gary's hand. "These are from a house plant—*grape* ivy," he said, looking quizzically at Gary, then at Ricky.

"April Fool," Ricky told Gary, a wide grin spreading across his face. He shoved his hair back out of his eyes.

Everyone laughed, mainly because of the shocked look on Gary's face. "He got you," Suki told Gary, pulling him back to his seat. "He got you that time." Gary forced a smile to his face, more for Suki's sake than anyone else's.

"Take your seats. Afraid this is going to be a short meeting," Mr. Abner said, walking over to the window and looking out at the parking lot.

Everyone became silent. What did he mean? He had a very serious look on his normally cheerful face.

"I have a personal emergency back home in Nashville," he told them, still looking out the window. "I have to go home this weekend. So I won't be able to take you on the overnight Saturday."

Suki and Ricky groaned out loud. No one else made a sound. Della looked at Gary, then down at the floor, disappointed.

"We'll have to postpone it," Mr. Abner said, turning around and sitting on the window ledge. "But there'll still be time. It's only May. We'll reschedule it when I get back. Okay?"

Everyone muttered agreement.

"I've got to run," Mr. Abner said, glancing up at the wall clock over his desk. "Sorry about this. See you guys next week." He hurried out the door with even longer strides than usual, a worried, preoccupied look on his face.

Della and her friends sat in silence until he was gone. "What a shame," Della said, starting to get up.

"Saturday's supposed to be a beautiful day too," Pete said. "At least, that's what they said on the radio."

They all started to get up.

"Hey—wait. I've got an idea," Suki said, motioning for the others to come back. "Listen. Really. I've got a good idea. Let's *go* on the overnight."

"What?" Maia cried. "Suki, what do you mean?"

"Let's go on the overnight anyway. You know. Without Abner."

"Go without an advisor?" Maia seemed to be appalled by the idea. "My parents would kill me! I'd be grounded for life. For *two* lifetimes!"

"They'll never know," Suki said.

"Yeah. Right," Ricky cried enthusiastically. "Neat idea! We'll go by ourselves. It'll be terrific. No one to bother us or tell us what to do." He stared at Suki. "Who wants to share my tent?"

"Get real, Schorr," Suki said, rolling her eyes. "You won't get *mosquitoes* to share your tent!"

Everyone else laughed. Ricky looked really hurt.

"Our parents will think we're being chaperoned. They'll think Abner is with us," Suki said, lowering her voice even though there was no one around to overhear. "And what they don't know won't hurt 'em." She put a hand on Gary's arm. "What do you think? You're the club president."

"Well—" Gary started.

"But my parents will kill me!" Maia protested.

"I think it's a good idea," Pete said, looking at Della. "After all, we're very responsible. We're not going to do anything crazy, right?"

Suki grinned up at Gary. "Not if we can help it," she said meaningfully.

"What do you think, Della?" Pete asked.

Della was eager to go. "It could be fun," she said. "We really don't need Abner." It could be a lot of fun, she thought. Especially if I can pry Gary away from Suki long enough to make up with him.

"What do you say, Gary?" Suki demanded.

"Well . . . okay." He grinned at her. "Let's do it. Let's go Saturday morning, just as we planned."

That brought a cheer—from everyone except Maia.

"I can't," she said unhappily. "If my parents ever found out . . ."

"They won't find out, Maia," Della said. "Really. Everything will be fine. We'll have a great time, even better than if we had a chaperone. We'll come home Sunday morning as scheduled. And none of our parents will ever know."

"You promise?" Maia asked Della, her voice filled with doubt.

"I promise," Della told her. "Trust me, Maia. Nothing bad will happen."

chapter

2

"*D*id you pack a toothbrush? What about your toothbrush?"

Della silently counted to three. Then, in a controlled voice, she said, "Yes, Mom. I packed my toothbrush. Do you think I should take my hair dryer too? And another three or four changes of clothing? It *is* overnight, after all."

"No need to be sarcastic," Mrs. O'Connor said, squeezing Della's rolled-up sleeping bag. "Is this rolled tightly enough? Will you be able to carry it, do you think?" Della's mother was short and very thin—she weighed just under one hundred pounds—and she always moved and talked quickly, asking ten questions in the time it took most people to ask one. She reminded Della of a butterfly fluttering from flower to flower without ever resting. Now, Saturday morning, she was busily fluttering around Della's room as Della prepared for the overnight.

"Mom, what are you so uptight about?" Della asked. "We used to camp out a lot when Dad was still here.'' She felt a sudden pang of regret. Maybe she shouldn't have mentioned her father so casually. Her parents had divorced two years before, and her father had immediately remarried.

Her mother didn't react. She was too busy squeezing the sleeping bag. ''This Mr. Abner,'' she said. ''You never talk much about him.''

''That's because I don't have him for any classes. He's just our club advisor. He's great. Really. You shouldn't worry, Mom.''

''But why Fear Island?'' Mrs. O'Connor asked. ''It's such a creepy place.''

''Well, that's the point,'' Della said, walking over to the mirror and pulling the hairbrush down through her long, straight hair even though it didn't need it. ''It's supposed to be exciting, see.''

''But Fear Island . . . There've been such awful stories.'' Her mother straightened some books on a shelf and then fluffed the pillow on Della's bed.

Fear Island was a small, uninhabited island, covered with pine trees, in the center of the lake behind the Fear Street Woods. Even though it was a perfect spot for picnics and camping, and only a few minutes' boat ride across the lake, few people ventured there because of the dreadful stories about it.

Some said that strange animal mutations, hideous, dangerous creatures that didn't exist anywhere else, roamed the woods. Others said the island was infected with poisonous snakes. And there were stories that the island had been used long ago as an Indian burial ground, and that ghosts walked the woods at night, seeking revenge for their fate.

Della didn't really believe any of the stories. She

was sure they were made up by campers to discourage others from crowding onto the island. But they certainly added an air of adventure to an overnight there.

"We didn't want to camp in a boring state park," Della told her mother. "We wanted to be somewhere more exciting."

"Well, I hope it isn't *too* exciting," her mother said, walking up behind her and straightening the bottom of her sweatshirt. "If anything bad happens, you'll call me right away, right?"

Della spun around, laughing. "Call you? On what? I'll tell you what—I'll send up a smoke signal, okay?"

"You're not funny," Mrs. O'Connor said. But she was laughing too.

The honking of a car horn from the driveway ended their conversation. "That's Pete," Della told her mother. She lifted her backpack onto her shoulders and picked up the blue sleeping bag.

"Who's Pete?" her mother asked suspiciously. She wasn't used to the fact that Gary wasn't always hanging around.

"A boy from the club." Della leaned over, kissed her mother on the cheek, and lumbered out the door under the weight of the bulging backpack.

She waved to Pete, who climbed out of the blue Subaru station wagon to help her with her stuff. He was wearing tan chinos and a plaid flannel pullover shirt. "Hi," he said, pulling up the rear door. "Nice day." The sun was high in a solid blue sky.

"Yeah. It's so peaceful out here."

"Peaceful?" He looked confused.

"My mother isn't out here asking a million questions."

He laughed. He has such perfect teeth, she thought. Too perfect.

Then she scolded herself for being so hard on him. He was a nice guy, after all. It was nice of him to offer her a ride to the lake. He couldn't help it if his teeth were too straight, and his nose was too straight and perfect, and his hair was too smooth, and he dressed better than anyone else.

He really seemed to like her. Maybe, she thought as she climbed into the front seat beside him, she should try to like him too.

But their conversation as they headed to the lake was awkward. Pete was telling her about some camping trip he had gone on with his family, but she couldn't concentrate. His voice kept drifting in and out of her consciousness. She was thinking about Gary. She kept thinking of what she would say to him, how she would start to make up with him when they were alone together in the woods.

"Did you?" Pete asked.

"Huh?" She realized she hadn't heard a word he'd said for at least a mile.

"Did you and Gary break up?" He stared straight ahead at the road.

"Well, yeah. I guess. I mean no. I don't know."

Pete laughed uncomfortably. "Should I choose one of the above?"

"Sorry," Della said. The question had gotten her all flustered. "Gary and I . . . I mean, we haven't really settled things."

"Oh." Pete didn't hide his disappointment. "This overnight should be fun," he said, changing the subject. "You're not scared about spending the night on Fear Island, are you?"

"No. I don't think so."

"Stick with me. I'll protect you," he said in an exaggerated, deep he-man voice.

"Protect me from what? From Ricky's bad jokes?"

"I think he's kind of funny," Pete admitted, turning down Fear Street and heading toward the woods. "In a gross, unfunny kind of way."

The car bumped over the road, which ended at the edge of the Fear Street Woods, fifty yards or so from the water. "Everyone's here already," Della said. Pete honked the horn as the others came into view.

She could see Gary and Ricky arguing about something. Maia was sitting by the water. Suki was standing next to Gary. Pete stopped the car and cut the engine. Della could see backpacks and sleeping bags piled up beside the two canoes Gary had brought.

She waved to her friends and helped Pete carry their equipment from the back of the station wagon. "The lake looks so pretty today," she said. The water was very still and very blue, reflecting the clear sky above. Two ducks squawked and bobbed their heads as they swam near the shore. Fear Island was a low mound of green on the horizon.

"Okay. We're all here. We can get going," Gary said, looking at Della. He was wearing a faded denim jacket over a red T-shirt. His blond, wavy hair sparkled like gold in the sun.

He looks terrific, she thought. She gave him a

warm smile, and he smiled back. "Gary, I want—" she started.

But Suki quickly stepped in front of her. "I've never paddled a canoe. Will you show me how?" she asked Gary in a kittenish voice.

"Sure," he told her. "Just sit in the middle and watch. The person in the middle doesn't paddle."

"I'll take this canoe. You guys can all take that one," Ricky said. He jumped into the one on the left and stretched out on his back, taking up the whole canoe.

"Very funny, Schorr. Remind us to laugh later," Suki said.

Della had to smile at Suki's outfit. It wasn't exactly outdoorsy. Her jeans had silver studs up the pants legs. She wore a long black T-shirt with a shorter white Guns-N'-Roses T-shirt on top of it. As usual, she had four different earrings in each ear.

"Hi, Della. I'm here." Maia hurried over to Della, smiling but looking worried just the same.

"Great," Della said. "Did your parents give you a hard time?"

"No. Not really," Maia said. "Only, when they dropped me off here, they wouldn't leave. They wanted to talk to Mr. Abner first."

"Oh, no. What did you do?"

"Schorr made a few jokes, and they decided they'd rather go," Suki cracked.

"Give me a break," Ricky cried, still lying in the canoe. "Hey—where's the gas pedal in this thing?"

"They changed their minds," Maia told Della. "But I just know they're going to find out what we're doing." She nervously squeezed her hands into tight fists at her sides.

"Don't be ridiculous," Della said. "How will they ever find out?"

A few minutes later they were paddling, three to a canoe, over the still blue lake, out to Fear Island. "The water's so clear today, you can see fish in there," Pete said, leaning over the side and peering down.

The canoe started to tip. "Oh. Sorry about that." He straightened and continued to paddle.

"Going for a swim, Pete?" Ricky called from the other boat. "You didn't bring your rubber-ducky inner tube!"

No one laughed. The two canoes cut through the water side by side. Pete and Della paddled one canoe with Maia sitting in the middle. Gary and Ricky paddled the other, with Suki practically sitting in Gary's lap.

Is she going to leave him alone for one second? Della asked herself. She was determined to talk to Gary as soon as possible. She had rehearsed over and over what she wanted to say. She knew he would want to go back to her once she talked with him, once she apologized. Suki could just find someone else. That wouldn't be a problem for her.

Patient, be patient, Della repeated silently as she rowed. But it was so hard to wait. Why was there so much waiting in life? Even when you were supposed to be having a good time, you spent most of it waiting!

The slap of the paddles against the water was the only sound now. Della began to feel really warm despite the cool air. She moved her paddle smoothly, keeping in rhythm with Pete's paddle. The island grew larger as they glided closer. She could make out a rocky beach in front of a line of pine trees. A few more minutes . . .

"Whooa!" She heard Ricky cry out and looked up to see him standing up in the other canoe. His eyes were wide and he was covering his mouth with his hand. The boat tipped from side to side.

"Sit down!" Gary yelled to him.

"Seasick! Seasick!" Ricky shouted, struggling to stay on his feet as the canoe bobbed violently beneath him.

"Don't be a dork. You're going to tip us over!" Suki cried, very alarmed.

Ricky held his paddle up over his head with one hand and kept his other hand over his mouth. "Seasick! Ulllp! Seasick!"

"Sit down and be seasick!" Gary yelled again.

"Oh. Good idea." Ricky plopped back down in his place. He grinned at Gary and Suki. He had been faking the whole thing.

"Not funny, Schorr," Gary said, shaking his head.

"You should change your name to that," Suki added, still looking shaken. "Not-Funny Schorr."

"Come on," Ricky said, resuming his paddling. "You guys got a laugh out of it, didn't you? Didn't you?"

They didn't answer him.

The canoes began to bob up and down as the current became stronger near the island's shore. Della was enjoying the ride, the feel of the paddle in her hands pulling the canoe forward with each stroke, the cool wind against her face, the splash and tumble of the rolling water.

A few minutes later they were pulling the canoes onto the beach. "I want to keep on going," she said to no one in particular. "It felt so good on the water."

"It feels much better to be on dry land," Suki said. "Hey!" She let go of the canoe to examine her hand. She had broken one of her long, purple press-on nails. "Now what am I going to do? I didn't pack any replacements," she grumbled.

"I guess that's what's called roughing it," Ricky cracked.

She stuck out her tongue at him.

Suki walked alongside the others, examining her broken nail as they pulled the canoes across the narrow strip of pebbles to where the trees began. "They should be okay here," Gary said, dropping the front of his canoe at the foot of a tall pine tree.

"Is it lunchtime yet?" Ricky asked. "Can we order a pizza or something?"

"Good idea. Why don't you go get it?" Suki said, throwing the broken nail onto the sand. "We'll wait here for you."

Ricky looked hurt.

"I love campfires and making hot dogs over a fire," Maia said, looking a lot more cheerful.

"Hey—it's still morning, remember?" Gary reminded them. "We've got a lot to do before it's campfire time. Come on. Pick up your packs and stuff. We've got to find a good campsite."

"Aye, aye, chief," Ricky said, giving Gary a backward salute.

Pete helped Della on with her backpack and

handed her sleeping bag up to her. She thanked him and hurried up to walk with Maia. Pete was being really sweet. Too sweet. She really didn't want to encourage him.

They walked along the beach for a while, keeping near the tree line. The sun was higher in the sky now and it was becoming really warm. Della looked up to see what was causing the loud, discordant squawking she heard. Two blue jays on a low tree limb seemed to be having an argument. "Look how big they are!" she said to Maia, pointing.

"Blue jays are the noisiest birds," Maia said disapprovingly. "They're not at all like bluebirds. Bluebirds are so sweet."

"Welcome to Nature Studies 101," Ricky interrupted.

"Come on, Ricky," Della scolded. "Why'd you come on this trip if you don't like to look at nature?"

"To get close to *you*, babes," Ricky said, flashing her an evil grin. "You know, I brought a king-sized sleeping bag. Big enough for me—and a friend."

"What an irresistible invitation!" Della made a face and started walking faster. A dirt path led into the trees, and they followed it. It curved through thick woods, still deep with brown winter leaves. After a while they came to a circular clearing of tall grass and weeds.

"This looks good," Gary said, tossing the tent he'd been carrying over his shoulder to the ground. "Let's set up here."

They all gratefully removed their packs and placed them on the ground. There were two tents to be set up, one for the boys and one for the girls.

"No. Turn them around this way," Pete instructed after they had started to stretch the canvas over the poles they had put together. "The wind usually comes down from the north. So the backs of the tents should face north."

"Very impressive, Pete," Gary said, only half joking. He looked up at the sun, which was directly above them. "But how do we tell which way is north?"

"It's that way," Pete said, pointing. "I have a compass on my watch." He held up his wrist, displaying one of those calculator watches with a dozen different functions.

"Do you think Daniel Boone had one of those?" Ricky asked.

Once again, everyone ignored him. They worked to turn the tents around and get them tightly pegged to the ground. Then they set off in different directions to gather enough firewood to last the night.

Pete started to follow Della, but again she hurried to catch up with Maia. "This is kind of scary," Maia said, stepping carefully over a deep puddle.

"But fun," Della added. She was very excited, she realized, but she wasn't sure why. Maybe it was the fact that they were really on their own, with no adults in sight. Anything could happen. Anything. Just the six of them, alone in the woods for the night. It could be so romantic. . . .

She headed away from Maia and started in the direction Gary had gone off in. This is my chance to talk to him, she thought. She realized that her heart was pounding. Her mouth felt dry. She didn't think she'd be this nervous.

Gary must mean more to me than I let myself

admit, she thought. She stepped quickly over the dry brown leaves and fallen twigs, looking for him through the birch and pine trees.

It smelled so sweet and fresh in the woods. She couldn't wait to talk to him, to be with him again, to feel his arms around her. How could she have been so stupid as to lose her temper like that and break up with him? She didn't even remember now what the argument was about.

A squirrel stopped halfway down a tree trunk. It stared at her as she hurried past, then scampered over the leaves to the next tree.

"Gary, I want to apologize." Those were going to be her first words. No fancy introductions. No excuses or explanations. She'd just apologize and get it over with.

She stopped. There he was. She could see him through a gap in the trees. She stifled a horrified gasp.

He was leaning back against a broad tree trunk. Suki was pressed against him. They had their arms wrapped tightly around each other. Their eyes were closed. They were locked together in a long, long kiss.

chapter
3

*N*o one was surprised later that afternoon when Ricky pulled a gun from his pack.

"Come on, guys—everybody take one." He pulled out five more pistols, one at a time.

"Great! Let's do it!" Pete cried enthusiastically.

"Okay!" Gary was just as gung ho. He grabbed a gun from Ricky and pretended to fire it at Pete. Pete hit the ground and pretended to retaliate with his gun.

The three girls groaned in unison.

"Not another ZAP war," Della sighed.

"I hate war games," Suki complained. "They're so . . . competitive."

What a long word for her, Della thought bitterly. In the hours since she had seen Suki and Gary in the woods, her hurt had turned to anger.

"I've never played," Maia said. "Do you divide into teams, or is it every man for himself?"

"We'll do teams," Ricky said, pulling out the paint for the ZAP guns.

"Include me out," Suki said.

"Come on, girls. It'll be fun," Gary pleaded. "A bunch of us had a ZAP war a few weeks ago in Shadyside Park. We ended up covered in paint. It was hilarious."

"Sounds like a real laugh riot," Suki said sarcastically.

"Okay. I'm game," Della said, suddenly changing her mind. If Suki was against it, then she was going to be for it! Let Gary see who was the better sport.

"Me too, I guess," Maia said, looking at Della for reassurance.

"Great!" Gary cried. "Come on, Suki." He put a hand on her shoulder. "You're the only holdout."

"I told you, I don't like war games," Suki insisted, pulling away from Gary.

"It's not a war. Think of it as just a game—with shooting," Ricky suggested.

Suki glared at him and poked his chubby stomach with her finger. "Will I get a chance to shoot *you* with paint, Schorr?"

"Yeah. I guess," Ricky said. "Ooh. Poke me again. I love it!"

"Shut up!" Suki said, making a fist and shaking it at Ricky playfully. "Okay, you win. I'll play. But only because I'll get to massacre you, Schorr."

"Girls against the boys," Pete suggested.

"Good deal," Gary agreed quickly.

Della was disappointed. She wanted to be on Gary's team. And she didn't want to be on the same team with Suki.

Ricky was busy loading the ZAP guns with paint, yellow for the girls, red for the boys. "Remember, two hits and you're a prisoner. Three hits and you're dead," he said seriously.

"I should've known you were bringing these," Pete said, rolling his loaded gun around in his hand. "Your backpack was so much bigger than everyone else's."

"I bring them everywhere," Ricky said. "I brought them to my cousin's wedding!"

"How long are we going to play?" Maia asked, looking at her watch. "Not when it's dark, are we?"

"We'll have creamed them by then," Suki said, taking her loaded ZAP gun from Ricky. She squirted a stream of yellow paint into the air. Ricky glared at her. "Just testing," she said.

"No shooting for ten minutes," Ricky said. "That gives us time to scatter and take positions."

ZAP wars were the only times Ricky was ever serious. Della decided she liked him better this way, not cracking horrible jokes, not trying so desperately hard to be funny. Unfortunately, according to Gary, Ricky wasn't too good at the game. He made too big a target and was always getting hit.

A shadow passed over the campsite. Della looked up at the sky. A few puffy gray clouds interrupted the clear blue. The air suddenly got colder.

The boys left camp first, traveling south in a group. The girls decided to wait a few minutes and then go west. Then they'd split up and circle in on the boys. After the boys left, laughing and joking, Suki changed into an olive-green sweater, saying it was better camouflage.

Wow, another big word. Two in one day, Della thought. She never had liked Suki. Actually, she had never thought much about her at all. They didn't hang out with the same crowds. But now Della had plenty of reason to think about Suki, and plenty of reason to dislike her.

Or was she being unfair? She had broken up with Gary, after all. Sort of.

"Come on. Let's get going," Maia said. The pistol looked really big and out of place in her little hand.

They started walking together into the woods. "This is kind of sexy," Suki said.

"Huh? Sexy?" Della didn't get it.

"Yeah. You know. Hunting and being hunted."

"Oh."

"It's kind of exciting," Suki said, carefully stepping over a fallen tree limb.

A gust of wind made the new green leaves on the trees whisper and shake. A large cloud rolled over the sun, and the woods suddenly grew dark.

"Is the paint washable?" Maia asked. Her enthusiasm was short-lived. She sounded like her old worried self again.

"Yes, of course," Della said sharply. "Ricky *told* us it was washable. It'll come right out."

Maia looked at her, recognizing the impatience in her voice. Della reminded herself that it was Suki she resented. She shouldn't take it out on Maia.

"Let's split up here and circle around," Suki said, gesturing with the large gray pistol.

"Okay," Della agreed quickly. She realized she was looking forward to being on her own, away from everyone.

"How do I find you if I get lost?" Maia asked, tugging at the sleeves of her sweatshirt.

"Walk away from the sun. East. And you'll be heading back toward camp," Della advised.

Maia looked up at the sun, as if to make sure it was still there. "Okay. See you later." She turned and walked off slowly through the trees, holding the pistol in front of her.

"Listen for footsteps," Della called after her. "No one will be able to come up behind you without making loud footsteps."

"Thanks!" Maia called back.

"She's such a little girl," Suki said quietly.

She didn't say it scornfully, but Della didn't like the idea of Suki putting down her friend. "She's okay," she told Suki, sounding angrier than she had intended.

"Gary's really nice," Suki said suddenly.

Della wasn't sure she had heard correctly.

Suki was staring into her eyes, as if searching for a reaction. Della forced her face to go blank. She wasn't going to give away her feelings to Suki so easily.

"You broke up with him, right?" Suki asked.

But before Della could answer—and what would she answer?—Suki headed off into the woods, pushing tall brambles out of her way so that she could pass through, her white Reebok hightops crunching over the dead leaves.

Della leaned against a smooth white tree trunk, watching Suki until she disappeared into the woods. What was she trying to prove, anyway? Was she trying to excuse her moving in on Gary so quickly? Was Suki challenging her? Was she trying to be friendly? Was she making fun of her?

Della wandered in the general direction the other

two girls had gone. Her mind was spinning, trying to figure out what Suki had intended with her surprising, casual remarks. She didn't really pay attention to where she was going. She completely forgot about the large plastic gun in her hand, the gun she was supposed to hold at the ready in case she came upon any of the boys.

The crunch of a footstep brought her back to reality. She spun around and ducked as a spray of red paint flew over her head. She dropped to her knees, raised her pistol, and fired without aiming.

"Hey!" she heard Ricky shout.

Peering through tall weeds, she saw him rubbing at a splotch of yellow paint on his sweatshirt. "Missed me!" she yelled, laughing. Keeping low, she darted to the left and ducked behind a broad tree trunk.

"Lucky hit!" Ricky shouted, running toward her at full speed. He fired, sending a stream of red paint up into the air. It died before it reached the tree.

Della fired back, once, twice, missing both times. Then she took off, running along a narrow path through the fir and pine trees.

She turned back in time to see Ricky, the splotch of yellow paint bright on the front of his dark sweatshirt, fall over a low stump and go sprawling face forward into the dirt. His ZAP gun bounced out of his hand and over the ground.

With a triumphant smile on her face, Della turned off the path and kept running. She pushed branches and brambles out of her way, moving at top speed. This was fun, she decided. Ricky would never find her now.

Suddenly, the clouds thickened and covered the

sun, making it nearly as dark as night in the dense woods. Screeching birds circled, then settled onto high tree limbs. The wind swirled dust and dry leaves around her sneakers.

She shivered, realizing that she hadn't kept track of the direction she was heading in.

Where am I?

She looked to the sun to gauge her position, but the dark clouds blotted it out almost completely. Some great advice I gave Maia about watching the sun, she told herself. Poor Maia was probably lost too.

"Hey—Maia!" she called aloud. She didn't care if the boys heard her or not.

There was no reply.

"Maia! Suki! Can you hear me?"

No reply.

The birds suddenly became silent. It was eerie, Della thought, as if someone had just turned them off, like turning off a TV set.

The silence was strange, unnatural.

"Now, don't start getting morbid," she scolded herself.

The wind shifted direction. A branch cracked somewhere behind her. She jumped as it hit the ground with a loud thud. She spun around, thinking someone was there.

"Maia? Suki?"

Where were they?

She turned and started walking back to camp. She wasn't sure it was the right direction, but it felt right. She had a pretty good sense of direction. Of course, she'd never been alone in the middle of the woods before.

There was one good thing about being on an island. The woods wouldn't go on forever. If she kept walking in a straight line, she'd eventually come out of them. But was she walking in a straight line? She couldn't tell.

The terrain sloped up, then down again. She realized she hadn't walked here before. Thick green moss grew up the side of a tilted old tree. Moss. Moss on a tree. It only grows on one side of the tree, she remembered. But which side? She stared at it. The north side? The east side? She couldn't remember.

"Maia? Suki? Anyone?"

Where *was* everyone?

A crunching sound. Behind her. A footstep?

She turned. No one there.

She turned back, walked past the mossy tree. The ground was hilly now, the inclines growing steeper as she walked.

Another crunching sound. Then another.

Someone was definitely following her. She didn't turn around. It was probably one of the boys, planning a sneak attack. But there was no such thing as a sneak attack when every step you took made a sound.

What should she do?

Count to ten, spin around, and fire.

She walked on, stepping through tall ferns bent low in the strong wind. Three . . . four . . . five . . .

The footsteps behind her were louder. Whoever it was was coming closer.

Eight . . . nine . . . ten!

She wheeled around, dropped to her knees, and pulled the trigger.

A stream of bright yellow paint flew through the air, splattering leaves and tree trunks, dripping down onto the dark ground.

A squirrel turned and darted away, making loud crunching sounds over the leaves as it ran.

A squirrel. It was only a squirrel.

She laughed out loud and sent another spray of paint high into the air.

She had been followed by a squirrel. And she had shot at it.

Good move, ace.

Guess I showed *him* not to mess with Della O'Connor.

She fired another shot at a tree trunk, missing by nearly a foot.

It was really dark now, but she didn't feel bad. The squirrel had cheered her up. She wasn't afraid anymore. It was silly to be afraid.

What was there to be afraid of?

She eased herself down a steep slope and began making her way across a flat area, the ground thick with fragrant pine needles and dried-up pinecones.

Suddenly, just a few feet ahead of her, someone stepped quickly out from behind a tree.

"Pete? Gary?"

She stopped short.

It wasn't one of her friends. It was a man she had never seen before. And he was moving toward her very quickly.

chapter

4

*H*e stopped a few feet in front of her, his hands in the pockets of his brown leather bomber jacket. His hair was sandy colored, cut very short. He smiled at her. He had a nice smile, she thought. In fact, he was really handsome, movie-star handsome.

She realized she was holding her breath. She let it out quickly. Her heart was pounding. "Hi," she said weakly. "You scared me. I didn't—"

His smile didn't fade. His dark eyes looked her up and down. "Sorry. You scared me too." His voice was smooth, mellow. She guessed he was about twenty-one or twenty-two.

"I didn't expect—"

"Me either," he said, shrugging, with his hands still in the jacket pockets.

He's really cute, she thought. What a smile!

"What are you doing here?" she blurted out. Then she quickly added, "I was looking for my friends. I seem to be lost. I mean—'' Why was she telling him this?

"Lost?" That seemed to amuse him. His smile grew wider, revealing straight, white teeth. He removed a hand from his jacket and swept it back over his short hair.

"Are you lost too?" she asked.

He laughed quietly to himself. "No, I don't think so."

"Oh." Then why was he here in the middle of Fear Island by himself?

"You from Shadyside?" he asked.

"Yeah. I'm on an overnight. We're camping out."

"Are we?" He laughed.

He's the most handsome guy I've ever seen, Della thought. Look at those dimples when he laughs. He really could be a model or something.

"Are you camping out too?" she asked.

"Sort of."

He was obviously playing a game with her, deliberately not telling her why he was there. "Like to answer questions?" she asked teasingly.

"Sure. Ask me anything. Want to know my social security number?" His eyes grew wide as he challenged her.

"No. I just—"

"Want to know my height and weight? My shoe size? My mother's maiden name?" He was talking rapidly, excitedly. She couldn't tell if he was joking or not.

"Yes, I think that would be very interesting," she said, making her own joke and watching to see his reaction.

He laughed. It was a warm, reassuring laugh. She felt drawn to him because of his laugh, because of his dark eyes, because of his clean, good looks.

"So why are you here in the middle of the woods on Fear Island?" she asked, leaning against a narrow tree trunk.

"Well, I came back, you see," he started.

"Back from college?"

"Yeah. Right. Back from college. I go to B.U. Up in Boston." He kicked at a thick, upraised root that curled along the dirt.

"But it's awfully early for school to be out," she said.

"Well . . . yeah. It's not out. I'm here on kind of a project. You know. About trees." He patted the trunk of the tree he was standing next to. "Lots of trees to study on the island. I'm doing my paper on tree reproduction."

"Reproduction?"

He grinned. "Yeah. You know what that is, don't you?"

They both laughed. "That sounds very . . . interesting," she said, staring into his eyes. Why did she feel like flirting with him? She didn't know a thing about him. She didn't even know his name.

"I'm Della. What's your name?"

"Della? That's funny. That's *my* name too!"

"Oh, get real . . ."

"No. I mean it." He raised a hand as if swearing he was telling the truth. He came a few steps closer. He was standing right in front of her now.

"I like your jacket," Della said. She reached out and touched the sleeve. "Real vinyl?"

He laughed. "You're very funny." His eyes

peered into hers, as if he were looking for something there. "A sense of humor is important, don't you think? I think so. Some people don't have a sense of humor. How do you deal with them? You know? What can you do about it? Sometimes it's the only way to reach someone. When you want to reach someone and they don't know where you're coming from. Follow my meaning?"

"No," she said, laughing.

He didn't laugh with her. He bit his lower lip. His face turned serious. He looked down at her. She realized for the first time how tall he was, about a foot taller than she.

"I'm talking about communication," he said, shouting the last word. "I'm talking about getting through to people when they don't want you to reach them. Know what I mean?"

"Yeah. I guess." He was starting to frighten her. What was this ridiculous rap about communication? He wasn't making any sense. Why was he getting so worked up?

She took a step back. She decided to change the subject. "So you like trees, huh?"

"Trees?" For a second he looked as if he didn't know what she was talking about. "Oh, yeah. Sure. I like your hair."

"It's all blown by the wind."

"I like that." He looked up at the sky. "Pretty cloudy. Hope it doesn't rain." He was calm again.

"Yeah."

He moved closer and fingered the sleeve of her sweatshirt. "Nice sweatshirt," he said.

"It's real vinyl." She could feel his breath on her

neck. She stepped back, but he didn't let go of her sleeve. "I guess I should get back."

"Back?"

"Back to my friends. They're probably wondering where I am."

"Where are you?" he asked. It didn't exactly sound like a joke. There was something unpleasant about the way he said it, something threatening.

"My friends. I have to get back to camp."

"Send this girl to camp," he said, unsmiling, staring into her eyes.

She noticed for the first time that he was sweating.

How weird, she thought. It's too cold to be sweating like that. His leather jacket can't be *that* warm!

"Nice to meet you, Della," she said, trying to keep it light, but eager now to get away from him.

He didn't say anything. He stood staring at her, expressionless. He seemed to be thinking hard, concentrating on something. "Are those *real* gold?" he asked, reaching for one of her hoop earrings.

"I don't know," she said, quickly backing away from him.

Suddenly, he grabbed her hair and held it tightly, pulling her head back.

"Hey!" she cried. "What are you doing?"

"I guess they *are*," he said. "Solid gold. You're a real *princess*, aren't you."

"No. Let go!" She tried not to let her panic sound in her voice, but she couldn't help it.

He tightened his grip on her hair.

"Come on—let me go. I'm *serious!*"

"Me too," he said in a low voice filled with menace.

Still pulling her hair with one hand, he grabbed her arm above the elbow with his other hand and pulled her against him. She could smell the leather of his jacket, the leather smell mixed with sweat.

"Hey—stop!" she pleaded. "You're *hurting* me!"

"Sorry, Princess." He tightened his grip.

She tried to pull away from him, but he was too strong. He dragged her up a brushy slope. At the top, she looked down into a deep ravine.

"What do you want?" she cried. "What are you going to do with me?"

chapter

5

Still holding her tightly with one arm, he unzipped his jacket. It was one of the loudest sounds Della had ever heard, and the most frightening.

"Pete! Gary!" she screamed.

He laughed quietly to himself. "No one can hear you," he whispered. He pushed her closer to the edge of the ravine.

"No, wait," she begged.

"What does waiting get you?" he said. His voice was smooth, calm; terrifyingly calm. "I've been waiting here. Too long. I've been waiting for a lot of things. Finally, I decided just to take something. Something for me. Know what I mean?" He was talking rapidly again, crazily, his eyes wild, spraying her with spittle as he leaned in close to her face.

"Just let go of me," she said, forcing her voice not to tremble. "I won't run away. I promise."

"I don't ask a lot. But I want *something*," he continued, ignoring her request. "That's what I told the old man. But he wouldn't listen. I couldn't communicate, see. That's what we're talking about. Communication. I found a way to communicate with him okay. I found a way. But it didn't do him any good. I mean, you don't learn a lesson if you're dead. Know where I'm coming from?''

"Uh . . . yes. Please let go.''

"You don't know what I'm talking about, do you? Well, you'd better not. Just play dumb, okay? *Okay?* You like me. I can tell. I think I can communicate with you. Yes?''

"Yes. No. You're hurting me!''

Breathing heavily, his chest heaving, he loosened his grip a little. Backing away, Della saw the silver chain around his neck, three silver skulls hanging from it. "Oh!'' she gasped. They were so ugly, so realistic, so evil looking.

He stared into her eyes. He seemed to be trying to read her thoughts.

"What do you want?'' she asked.

He didn't reply. He didn't blink. His silence was scarier than his wild talk.

She suddenly remembered the ZAP gun. She had shoved it into her back jeans pocket. She reached for it now, felt the barrel first, then grabbed the handle. She jerked her arm back, raised the gun, and fired.

A spray of yellow paint shot onto his forehead.

He sputtered, surprised, then cried out angrily and let go of her to wipe his forehead.

She took off, racing, stumbling, flying along the ground. Where was she going? She didn't know. She didn't care. She was getting away.

She tripped over an upraised root, but climbed

quickly to her feet. She was running blindly now, thick foliage rushing by in a blur.

And he was right behind her.

He lunged. His arms went around her legs. He tackled her.

She hit the ground hard. Her knee throbbed with pain, which shot up through the rest of her body.

His arms circled her waist.

Before she even realized she had been recaptured, he had pulled her to her feet. Angrily, he gave her a hard shove. He grabbed the ZAP gun from her hand and shoved the barrel into her back.

"Let me go! Let me go!" she wailed.

He stared at her, struggling to catch his breath, perspiration dripping down his forehead, down his smooth cheeks.

He pushed her ahead of him, back up to the top of the ravine. She struggled to break away, but he held on tightly, bending her arm behind her, poking the sharp nose of the ZAP gun into her back.

At the top of the ravine he stopped. He grabbed her by the shoulders and shook her hard. "You shouldn't have done that," he growled.

As he brought his face down closer, she pulled back both hands and gave him a fast, hard shove with all her might.

His eyes opened wide in surprise as he lost his footing.

"Hey!"

He tumbled backward. His feet flew out from under him as he began to topple down the side of the steep ravine.

His hands, desperately reaching for something to stop his fall, grabbed only air.

She closed her eyes.

She heard him scrape against the ground, once, twice. She heard him cry out. She heard a thud. A groan. And then silence.

It took three or four seconds at most.

It seemed like a year.

She opened her eyes. Everything seemed so much darker. The trees, the ground, the sky. She took a deep breath and held it. Sometimes that calmed her down.

This time it didn't work.

Her first instinct was to run. But she knew she couldn't run away until she had looked down to the bottom of the ravine.

The ground seemed to tilt. The trees seemed set at strange angles, warring with each other. She shook her head, trying to shake away the dizziness.

She looked down the ravine. It wasn't as deep or as steep as she had imagined.

He was lying at the bottom, his body twisted, his head in such a weird position, as if it had come off and been carelessly replaced by someone who didn't know which way a head was supposed to fit.

She took a couple of cautious steps down the slope.

He didn't move. His mouth was opened wide. His eyes were closed. His head was bent nearly sideways. It appeared to be resting on his shoulder.

"No!"

Had he broken his neck?

She felt sick. Everything started to spin. She sank to the ground and waited for the woods to stop moving.

What should I do? she wondered. This isn't really

happening—is it? Her mind was spinning faster than the trees. She wanted to wake up and forget this dream. She wanted to run away. She wanted to stop the panic she felt. If only she could think clearly . . .

Before she realized what she was doing, she was on her feet, tumbling and sliding down the side of the ravine. At the bottom she stood over the unmoving body, staring at the chain with its three silver skulls that seemed to stare back at her.

His mouth was locked open in an expression of horror. He seemed to be saying, *"You* did this to me. You killed me, Della."

"No!" she screamed. "Get up! Get up!"

She grabbed his arm and started to pull him up. The arm felt limp and lifeless. She dropped it, feeling a wave of revulsion roll up from her stomach.

"Get up! Get up!"

It was so dark, so hard to see. If only everything would stop spinning. If only she could breathe normally, think normally.

What should she do? What??

He's got to be alive, she thought. This can't be happening. It can't.

Her hands shaking, she sank to her knees in the dry leaves and reached for his hand. She moved her fingers around his wrist, trying to find a pulse.

Where is it? Where *is* it? Come on—there's *got* to be a pulse. . . .

Yes!

She found it. The soft, insistent thudding in his wrist, so fast, so strong. Yes. He had a pulse. He was alive. He—

No.

She shuddered. It was her own pulse she was feeling.

Her hands were shaking. She reached for his throat. She had seen this in movies. You find a pulse by pressing on the side of the throat.

The head rolled lifelessly back. She pressed hard against the throat. Nothing. She moved her fingers. Nothing.

Nothing. Nothing. Nothing.

She grabbed up his wrist.

Nothing.

"Ohh." She climbed to her feet, her hands covering her face.

He was dead. She had killed him.

Self-defense, she thought. It was self-defense.

But what did that matter? She had killed a man, another human being.

Now what?

Now her life would be *ruined*.

Now her parents would know she went on the overnight without Mr. Abner. Now *all* of the parents would know. She thought of Maia, of the promise she had made Maia that nothing would go wrong.

And now everything had gone wrong.

The whole town would know that she had killed a man. For the rest of her life she'd be haunted by this moment. Her life was ruined, *ruined*.

No.

Why ruin her life for this . . . this creep?

Why ruin all of their lives?

She turned her back to him so she could think better. Her mind was racing crazily, she realized. It was so hard to think clearly, to think in a straight line.

But she knew she had decided.

She wasn't going to tell anyone about him.

There was no reason to tell. And there was *every* reason not to tell.

It was an accident, anyway. Just an accident. He could have slipped and fallen down the ravine and hit his head and broken his neck or whatever he did to himself all by himself.

Suddenly she knew what she would do. It was easy, actually. And it was smart. She was being smart.

And she wasn't just protecting herself. She was protecting her friends. They didn't deserve to have their lives ruined forever because of this . . . accident.

She bent over and filled her arms with dry leaves, dead leaves from the winter just passed. Then she dropped the leaves over his legs. Another armful of leaves. She dropped them over his boots. Another armful.

It won't take long to cover him with leaves, she thought. Then I'll go back to camp and pretend this never happened.

She scooped up another armful of leaves. As she started to drop them onto his chest, she looked up to the top of the ravine.

Ricky and Maia were staring down at her.

chapter

6

"*H*e *attacked* me!" Della cried, struggling up the side of the steep ravine. "I didn't mean to do it! I mean, I didn't mean to push him. He just fell, you see. It was an accident!"

Maia looked even more upset than Della, but she hurried forward and put an arm around Della's shoulder, helping her away from the ravine and trying to calm her. "Take your time," she whispered into Della's ear. "Take your time. Tell it slowly."

"Who *is* that guy?" Ricky demanded, standing on the edge of the ravine, peering down at the half-covered body.

"I don't know," Della said, forcing herself to stop shaking, to stop breathing so hard and fast. "That's what I'm trying to tell you. He just came at me. He wanted to . . . he wanted to . . . I pushed him away, and he fell. He—He's dead. He's really dead."

Maia let go of her shoulder and backed away.

"Della, you promised me—" she started, but she was too upset to finish her sentence. "My parents—they're going to . . ."

Pete came up from behind Della and put a hand on her shoulder. "Take it easy. It's over now," he said gently. "We'll figure out what to do."

Della smiled at him. She was beginning to feel a little calmer.

"This is really gross," she heard Suki telling Gary. "I've never seen a dead body before."

"But who is he? What was he doing out here?" Ricky demanded, looking very serious for once.

"Just some creep," Della muttered, shivering.

"But what was he doing out here all by himself?" Ricky repeated, his voice high and whiny.

"Ricky, how should I know?" she snapped. "He wasn't a close personal friend, you know. He was some guy who attacked me in the woods. He didn't tell me his life story first."

"Sorry," Ricky said softly. "You don't have to shout."

Shout? She felt like screaming at the top of her lungs.

"Are you sure he's dead?" Gary asked suddenly.

"What?"

"Are you sure he's dead?"

"Well, yes," Della said, picturing again in her mind her frantic, unsuccessful attempts to find a pulse. Thinking about it, she began to feel dizzy again. She sat down on the ground, leaning back on her hands. closing her eyes.

"Maybe we should double-check," Gary said.

"I just don't believe this is happening," Maia

cried. "All of our lives wrecked because of a stupid overnight."

"Just *shut up*, Maia!" Della screamed, losing control, not caring.

"But my parents are going to *kill* me!" Maia insisted. Della looked up at her. Tears were streaming down her cheeks.

Why is *she* crying? Della wondered. How can *she* have the nerve to cry? *I'm* the one who just killed a man!

"Chill out, Maia," Suki said sharply. "This isn't going to do any of our reputations any good."

"I don't feel so well," Ricky said. "My stomach . . ." He ran into the trees.

"I'm going down there," Gary said.

"What for?" Suki grabbed his arm.

But he pulled out of her grasp and slid down the side of the ravine. "Wait—I'll go with you," Pete said. But he made no attempt to follow.

Della stood up and watched Gary make his way to the bottom of the ravine. The wind had picked up, blowing the leaves she had piled on top of the young man, making it look as if he were moving. Somewhere off in the distance she heard crows cawing loudly. The crows made her think of buzzards. She pictured large black buzzards voraciously attacking the stranger, pulling him apart.

She shook her head hard, trying to erase the hideous picture from her mind. Gary was bending over the body now, brushing away some of the leaves Della had piled on.

"He feels cold," Gary shouted up to them, his voice trembling, sounding higher than usual.

No one said anything. Ricky returned, sweating hard, looking very shaken.

"I can't find a pulse," Gary called up.

"What are we going to do?" Ricky asked, sitting down on the ground, crossing his legs and propping his head up with his hands.

"We're going to finish covering him with leaves," Suki said, as if it had all been decided.

"We are?" Maia asked, more hopeful than surprised. "We're going to pretend we don't know about this?"

"What do you think, Della?" Pete asked, standing very close to her, starting to put his arm around her shoulders, then hesitating.

"Can we keep a secret like this?" Della asked, staring off into the trees, not looking at them.

"We *have* to," Maia insisted.

"Yeah, we have to," Ricky repeated glumly, his head down.

Gary reappeared, breathing heavily, looking shaken. "No pulse at all," he said.

"We've decided to cover him up and pretend it didn't happen," Suki told Gary.

"I guess." Gary shook his head. "Anyone disagree with that plan?"

No one replied.

"Let's go," Gary said, looking at Pete.

"I'll help," Della said, starting after them.

"No." Pete held up a hand. "Gary and I can do this."

They disappeared down into the ravine. Della didn't watch, but she could hear the scratch and rustle of leaves as they buried the young man's body in them. She knew it was a sound she would never forget.

A few minutes later all six of them headed back to camp in silence. Somehow Della was surprised to find the tents, the backpacks, the equipment, and firewood all just as they'd left them. Her whole world had changed in that instant back on the edge of the ravine. She found herself expecting everything to be different now. It was reassuring, somehow, to see the campsite looking the same.

Maybe everything *will* go on as before, she thought. Maybe the secret will be left behind here on Fear Island and the memory of it will eventually fade.

"Let's pack up and get out of here," Suki said, picking up her backpack.

"Right," Maia agreed. "I don't want to spend another second on this horrible island."

"No, wait," Della insisted. "We can't go back now. Our parents will all want to know why we came back so early, why we didn't spend the night."

"She's right," Gary said quickly.

"You mean we have to spend the whole night here?" Maia cried. "No! I won't! I won't!" She picked up her backpack and angrily heaved it at the pile of firewood.

"Maia, if you don't chill out, we'll cover you with leaves too," Suki threatened.

Maia gasped. Ricky laughed. He was looking a little more like his usual self.

"Let's everybody try to stay calm," Gary said. "Della's right. We have to stay here till tomorrow. We have to make everything look like normal. We can't give our parents any reason to suspect that the overnight wasn't a great success."

"What a bummer," Suki muttered. "I don't think anyone's in the mood for this anymore."

"I know," Gary replied. "But we have no choice—do we? We have to stay."

"But I'm so cold," Maia whined.

"Let's get the fire going," Gary said. "A warm fire will make everyone feel better."

"A warm dinner will make *me* feel better," Ricky said. "Especially since I just blew lunch!"

They built a large fire and roasted hot dogs over it. Della was surprised to find that she hadn't lost her appetite. No one said much. Even Ricky ate in silence, hungrily wolfing down his food.

It was a clear, cool night. The wind gusted and swirled, making the campfire flicker and bend. Della looked up to find the sky filled with bright yellow and white stars. "How are you doing?" Pete asked, scooting down onto the blanket beside her.

"Okay, I guess." She smiled at him. He really was being nice to her. Gary and Suki sat across the campfire from her, sharing a blanket but not saying anything as they ate.

Maia sat as close to the fire as she could get. She was rubbing her hands together, trying to warm them. "I just can't get warmed up," she said, seeing Della and Pete staring at her.

"Guess no one wants to tell ghost stories around the fire tonight," Ricky quipped after they were finished eating. It was his first attempt at a joke, and it received the same silent reception most of his jokes received.

"I think we should get to sleep as early as possible," Maia said. "Then when we wake up, it'll be time to go home." She shook her head miserably, staring into the orange glow of the fire. "I just want it to be time to go home."

She stood up and started to drag her blanket toward the girls' tent.

"No—wait," Gary called, taking his arm off Suki's shoulder. "First we have to take an oath."

"Huh? What kind of oath?" Ricky asked, wrapped in his blanket so that only his face showed.

"An oath of secrecy," Gary said. "The secret of Fear Island must stay here forever. We all have to hold hands and swear to it."

The wind howled as the six of them stood solemnly in a circle. They each reached a hand forward over the fire. All six hands touched together.

Suki pulled her hand away. "This is stupid," she said.

"No, it isn't. A ceremony makes it official," Gary told her.

Suki rolled her eyes, but put her hand back with the others. They all leaned together, their faces orange in the firelight. "The secret shall be kept," Gary said slowly, his voice a whisper.

And as he said it, a rush of wind blew out the fire.

Maia screamed. It took a few seconds to get her calmed down. Pete and Suki quickly got the fire relit. Maia was the only one who had reacted, but everyone seemed pretty shaken now.

"At least there isn't a full moon," Ricky said. "We probably don't have to worry about werewolves." His joke was half-hearted. No one reacted.

They piled up their backpacks near the fire since

there was no room for them in the small tents. Then Della led Maia to the girls' tent. As she reached the opening, she turned and saw Gary wandering away from the campsite with Suki, their arms around each other's waists.

Inside the tent the air was warm and wet. Della began to unroll her sleeping bag, then stopped. Outside she could hear the wind and the rustling of leaves.

The rustling of leaves, leaves being dropped over a young man's body. Buried in leaves. In leaves. Buried in the rustling leaves.

"No!" She held her hands over her ears, but the sound of the rustling leaves didn't go away.

"You okay?" Maia asked, climbing into her sleeping bag fully dressed.

"What?" It was hard to hear Maia over the sound of the leaves. So many leaves, dry, brown leaves. piled so high.

"I asked if you're okay."

"Yeah, sure. I guess."

"We never should have come here," Maia said. "I knew we never should have done this." She turned her head away from Della.

Della didn't say anything. She finished unrolling her sleeping bag, listening to the wind and the leaves, thinking about the young man, feeling his forehead pressed against her cheek again, smelling the leather of his bomber jacket, then seeing him fall backward as she shoved him, shoved him, shoved him to his death.

She forced herself to think about something else. Gary. No. She couldn't think about Gary either. He was off in the woods now, making out with Suki.

Why had she agreed to go on this overnight? The whole point was to try to make things up with Gary. But that was out of the question now. Finished. Done. Done for.

Like the young man in the woods.

Stop it, Della. Stop thinking about it.

No, I can't. I can't. I'll never be able to stop.

A few hours later she awoke from a dreamless sleep. Her arm tingled and felt numb. She realized she'd been sleeping on it. She pulled it out of the sleeping bag and tried to shake it back to life.

Her face felt wet and cold. Everything felt damp. She sat up, her eyes adjusting to the darkness. Maia was asleep, curled deep in her sleeping bag. Suki was asleep too, breathing noisily through her open mouth. When did she come in?

Della swept a hand back through her hair. Wet, wet, wet. Weren't tents supposed to keep out the dew?

She heard a sound just outside the tent. A chill ran down her back. Was someone out there?

She listened.

The wind had died down. It was silent now.

A crackling twig broke the silence. Was it a footstep? She heard a scraping sound. Yes. Someone was there.

Was anyone else awake?

She listened. Another crackling noise, like a footstep on twigs or dry leaves.

She pulled herself up, her arm still tingling. She was wide awake now.

"Maia! Suki! Wake up!" she whispered. "Maia—please! Somebody—wake up!"

Her two tentmates stirred. "What time is it?" Maia finally asked, her voice raspy from sleep.

"Ssshh," Della warned. "Listen. I think there's someone out there."

That startled Suki and Maia into consciousness. They both climbed onto their knees. "Huh? Probably the wind," Suki whispered. But she looked as frightened as Maia.

"What should we do?" Maia asked, pulling her sleeping bag around her to keep warm.

"Sssh. Listen," Della whispered.

They heard a crunching sound. A sound like a shoe scraping over dirt. Then another sound.

What was that? A cough?

Della got to her knees and started making her way cautiously to the tent opening. Her side ached. Her neck felt stiff. Whoever said that sleeping on the ground was comfortable?

"Della—get back," Maia pleaded. "Where are you going?"

"To see who—or what—it is," Della whispered. "Are you coming with me?"

Suki ducked down into her sleeping bag, pulling it up around her head. Maia made no attempt to move.

"Looks like I'm going by myself," Della sighed.

"Go back to sleep." Suki's voice came out muffled through the sleeping bag. "This is all just a bad dream."

Another crunching sound outside the tent, this one a little louder, a little closer.

"Here. Take this." Maia, looking guilty, handed Della a flashlight.

Holding the flashlight in one hand, Della struggled into her sneakers. She hesitated at the tent opening, then stepped out, shining the flashlight in a quick circle around the campsite.

No one there.

She took another step out of the tent. The fire had nearly burned out, red-blue embers crackling weakly in front of her. She stopped and listened.

A footstep. Just beyond the boys' tent.

"Who's there?" she called, but her voice came out softly. She knew it didn't carry past the tents.

She heard another footstep.

"Anybody there?" A little louder this time.

Keeping the light ahead of her and down low, she walked past the boys' tent, stepping gingerly since her laces were untied. She was at the edge of the clearing now. There was no wind at all. The only sound was that of her breathing. And of another footstep over dry leaves.

She took a few steps into the trees. "Who's there?" She shined the flashlight in a wide circle.

She shivered, more from fear than from the cold. What am I doing out here? she asked herself. Who do I think I'll find? Why am I being so brave?

Shivering again, she turned back.

It was probably just some animal anyway, she thought.

Of all the stupid things. Wandering off into the woods in the middle of the night, chasing after a stupid animal. I'm losing my mind, she thought.

She stepped carefully past the fire and was about to climb back into the girls' tent when something caught her eye. The backpacks. They had been piled so neatly by the fire. Now they were scattered on the ground.

Had someone knocked them over?

She took a few steps toward them and shined the flashlight on them. They didn't seem to have been opened.

No. It must have been the wind. Or maybe an animal. A raccoon searching for food. That's all. The footsteps she heard heading into the woods—they must have been the same raccoon.

Maia and Suki were sitting up by the tent opening, nervously awaiting her return. "Just a raccoon, I guess," Della said with a shrug.

"I knew it," Suki said, shaking her head. She slid back down into her sleeping bag.

"Thank goodness," Maia breathed in relief.

Della kicked off the sneakers and slid back into the sleeping bag. It was cold in there now. She knew it would take a long while to warm it up. She listened. But now all she could hear was Suki's loud breathing.

She listened to Suki's snores and Maia's tossing and turning for the rest of the night. She couldn't get back to sleep.

In the morning they all emerged groggy and stiff, like bears coming out of a winter-long hibernation. Maia seemed constantly on the verge of tears, although she never gave in and cried.

They ate a quick breakfast and packed up in near silence, eager to get away from the island, eager to end the overnight, eager not to see each other for a while, to be able to go off somewhere and think silently, by themselves, about what had happened.

The red morning sun was still climbing over the trees when they stepped out of the woods and onto the rocky beach. The lake looked flat and purple in the morning light. The air was clear enough for them to see the town stretching along the bank on the other side of the water.

"Oh no! My backpack!" Ricky cried. "I left it back there." He turned and headed back to the campsight, running at full speed.

The others hurried toward where they had left the canoes, their sneakers crunching over the pebbles.

A few seconds later they all stopped. And stared.

"The canoes!" Della said.

They were gone.

"Oh no!" Maia cried. "We're trapped here!"

chapter

7

"Someone must have taken them," Della said. "I know this is where we left them." She shifted the heavy backpack on her shoulders and looked across the lake to town. It was so close, but so far away.

"Now, don't anybody panic," Gary said, looking very worried.

"Don't panic? What do you *mean,* don't panic!" Maia cried, her face red, her eyes wide with fear. "Who could have done this? What are we going to do? I've got to get home! My parents will *kill* me!"

"We won't be here long. When we don't get home on time, they'll send somebody to look for us," Gary said.

That was supposed to reassure them, but it didn't reassure Maia at all. "Then everyone will know that we came here without Mr. Abner!" she cried.

"Are you sure this is where we left them?" Suki asked, kicking at the sand.

"Yes, of course," Gary said. "Look. You can see the tracks in the sand."

"So somebody had to steal them," Della said quietly. She thought of the dead young man buried in the leaves. They were trapped on the island, trapped with him.

"What's going on?" Ricky called, lumbering up to them, dragging his backpack.

"The canoes—" Maia started.

"Oh no." Ricky turned white. "Oh, wow. I'm sorry. I moved the canoes."

"You *what?*"

"Why?"

A guilty grin spread over Ricky's face. He backed away from them, dropped his backpack on the sand and raised his hands as if preparing to fend off an attack. "It was supposed to be a joke. I did it yesterday, before the . . . uh . . . accident."

"I don't believe this." Suki scowled at Ricky. "You've got a great sense of humor, Schorr."

"I'm sorry. It was just a practical joke. Yesterday, I doubled back during the ZAP war and moved them," Ricky said. "So sue me. When I did it, I didn't know Della was going to kill a guy!"

Della gasped. "Ricky—"

"Give her a break, Schorr," Pete said quickly.

"Give us all a break," Gary said impatiently. "We all just want to get away from here. Where'd you hide the canoes?"

"Right over here." They followed Ricky about a hundred yards down the beach. The canoes were resting in some tall weeds behind a low dune.

"You really are a dork, Schorr," Suki said, looking at him as if he were a piece of dirt.

"I said I was sorry." He shrugged.

They pulled the canoes to the water, tossed their equipment in, and climbed in. The trip back to town seemed to take forever. No one talked. No one looked back at Fear Island.

One day later and we're all different people, Della thought. We all have a secret now. We all have a nightmare that we share, that we must hide.

She looked at Maia. Her auburn hair was a mess of matted-down tangles. Her eyes were red-rimmed, with dark circles around them. She looked as if she'd been crying all night. Pete, who was always so perfectly neat, was wearing a stained and wrinkled sweatshirt. His unbrushed hair fell down over his eyes.

The occupants of the other canoe looked just as worn out. Suki's spiked hair was plastered flat against her head. She hadn't even tried to comb it. Her face was pale, white as cake flour, as if all her blood had been drained. Ricky paddled silently in the rear of the canoe, breathing heavily, sweat dripping down his face despite the cool morning air. Only Gary looked almost normal, except for the tense, worried look on his face as he paddled rhythmically, never moving his eyes from the approaching shore.

I'm going to be home soon, Della thought. But it isn't going to be the same. Nothing is ever going to be the same again.

The slap of the paddles against the water gave way in her mind to the sound of rustling leaves. Again she saw the dry brown leaves being piled onto the lifeless form in the ravine. The leaves were everywhere, so dry, so dead. She looked down.

The lake was filled with them, filled with dead leaves, filled with death.

"Della—are you okay?" Pete's voice interrupted her thoughts. The rustling leaves vanished, replaced by the sound of the paddles and the water lapping against the sides of the canoe.

"Yes. I'm okay. I was just . . . thinking." She forced a smile. She knew it wasn't terribly convincing.

"Everything will be okay," Pete said. "You're almost home."

Almost home. Maybe I *will* feel better when I get home, Della thought.

But when, less than an hour later, she pulled open the back door and saw her mother dressed for church, finishing breakfast at the kitchen counter, she was overcome by a feeling of dread.

How could Della face her?

"Well?" Mrs. O'Connor asked, after tilting the coffee cup to her mouth to get the last drop. "How was it? You're home so early."

"Yeah. Well, we got up early," Della managed to say. She wondered if her mother could see how nervous she was. Mrs. O'Connor was usually a mind reader. She could read more into Della's eyes and expressions than was scientifically possible.

"You look like you didn't get much sleep last night." Her mother shook her head disapprovingly.

"Not much," Della said. She walked to the refrigerator and took out a carton of orange juice. She had a sudden urge to cry. She hoped that maybe, just maybe, an activity like getting orange juice for herself would help her keep control.

But how can I keep control? I killed a man last night!

Did her mother see her hand shaking as she poured the juice into a glass? No.

"Guess you don't want to come to church with me," her mother said.

"I'm going to go to bed. I could sleep for a week," Della told her.

"Was it fun?" Mrs. O'Connor asked, standing up and straightening her dress.

"Kind of," Della said, drinking the orange juice at the sink, keeping her back to her mother.

"Were you really up the whole night?" Mrs. O'Connor asked.

"No. Not the whole night."

"Want breakfast?"

"No. I don't think so."

"Did you talk to Gary?" Her mother knew Della hated questions about her boyfriends, but that never stopped her.

"Not too much." Della drank half the glass. She poured the rest in the sink.

"I was just asking," Mrs. O'Connor said with a shrug.

Ask me if I killed somebody last night, Della thought.

"You look exhausted," her mother said, frowning with concern.

I'm going to tell her everything, Della decided. I can't keep it in. I just can't. "Mom, I—"

"Yeah?" She was halfway out the door.

Della hesitated.

"What is it, Della?"

"See you later," she said.

The door closed behind her.

Della slept all morning and most of the afternoon. When she came downstairs a little before four, her mother was out. She made herself a tuna sandwich and ate it hungrily, washing it down with a Coke.

She felt a little better. All of that sleep helped a lot.

Taking a bowl of potato chips with her, she went back up to her room and did some Government homework. To her surprise, she was able to concentrate on the chapter she was reading. She thought about the young man in the ravine only once or twice, and even then it seemed like a distant memory, like something that had happened and was over.

When her mother got home, Della realized she no longer had the urge to tell her what had happened. At dinner she told her some stories about the overnight, some of them made up, some of them true. She told her about the ZAP war, about how good the hot dogs tasted over the open fire, how Ricky had hidden the canoes and how alarmed they were about it.

I may be able to do this after all, she thought. I may be able to put it behind me and go on with my life.

She began to feel confident, relaxed, almost good about herself—until the phone rang at seven-thirty, and she picked up and heard Maia's trembling voice.

"Della, can you come over? I'm not doing so well."

"What do you mean? Are you sick?"

"No. It's just—well, I'm sure my parents suspect something."

Della suddenly had a cold feeling on the back of her neck. Her neck muscles tightened. "Maia, you didn't tell them anything, did you?"

"No, of course not," Maia replied quickly, her voice tense and high. "Of course not, Della. But I think they suspect . . . I mean, I just have a hunch. And I don't—I mean, I don't know how much longer I can—"

"Okay. Try to calm down," Della said, sounding irritated when she meant to sound comforting. "I'll be right over."

"Thanks, Della. Hurry. Please."

Della hung up, feeling more annoyed than sympathetic. It seemed to her that Maia wasn't even trying to get over this. Well, maybe she was. Maybe she was doing the best she could.

In a way, she had gotten Maia into this mess. Maia wouldn't have even gone on the overnight if she hadn't urged her so strongly.

I've got to stop thinking about her so harshly, Della decided. I'll go over there and give her a pep talk, make her feel better. That's what friends are for, after all.

Friends.

Were her friends going to come through for her? Were they going to keep the secret as they had vowed?

They *had* to, Della decided. They *had* to.

She slipped into a clean pair of jeans and a light sweater, brushed her hair until it fell straight and smooth behind her shoulders, put on a little clear lip gloss, and then looked around the room for her wallet. It wasn't on her desk. It wasn't on the shelf by the door, where she usually kept it.

My wallet, she thought. When did I have it last? Did I bring it on the overnight? Yes. It had been in her backpack.

She hadn't unpacked her backpack, she realized. She had just tossed it down by the bed and forgotten about it.

She wanted to forget about it, of course. Now, as she picked it up and dumped the contents onto her bed, the old feeling of dread swept over her. The sound of the crackling dry leaves seemed to pour out of the backpack.

She tossed it to the floor and searched through the wrinkled clothing and toilet articles she had packed. Where was the wallet?

I know it was in there, she thought.

But it's gone.

Could someone have taken it? No. That was impossible.

Everything from the pack felt so cold. She had carried the chill of Fear Island home with her. And now she too felt chilled, pawing through her stuff again and still not finding the wallet.

How mysterious.

She decided to go to Maia's without it. Maia lived only a few blocks away in the North Hills section of town. Della told her mother she was going there to study, and headed out the door.

It was a warm night, almost balmy, a pleasant contrast to the night before. On a front lawn down the block a group of kids was playing baseball, even though it was already dark. A few doors down, Mrs.

Kinley was shouting for her son that it was time to come home, and was being completely ignored.

North Hills was such a quiet, peaceful neighborhood, the nicest neighborhood in Shadyside. For some reason, seeing the kids playing ball, walking past the large, quiet houses, past the manicured, carefully tended lawns, made Della feel sad. Somehow she didn't feel a part of that quiet, peaceful, respectable world anymore. Her secret made her an outsider.

Stop it, Della, she warned herself. Just stop it right now. It's natural that you feel sorry for yourself right now. But that will pass.

Maia opened her front door the instant Della rang the bell, and, without saying a word, pulled Della upstairs to her room and closed the door.

Della never could get over Maia's room. It looked like a little girl's room, with lacy white curtains on the windows, shelves of dolls, and stuffed animals everywhere.

"Maia—you look terrible!" Della cried, and then immediately regretted saying it. What a way to cheer someone up!

Maia burst into tears. "I keep crying, then stopping, crying then stopping," she sobbed. She pulled a handful of tissues from a box on her dresser and covered her face, blotting up the tears. When she took the tissues away, her face was bright red.

Della walked over and put her arm around Maia's shoulder. "Maia, everything will be okay. I promise," she said softly.

"You promised me before," Maia said, not looking at Della.

Della didn't know what to say. "What are you

worried about? Tell me in words," she said, leading Maia to the bed. Maia sank onto the gray and pink quilt. Della sat down in the small gray corduroy armchair across from the bed.

"My parents. I know they're suspicious."

"How do you know? What did they say to you?"

"Well . . . nothing exactly. But my mom looked at me funny."

"I don't blame her," Della said. "You don't exactly look your best. What did you tell them about the trip?"

"Not much. Just that I had a fun time and that I didn't spend the night making out in the boys' tent, and that it wasn't the wild orgy they imagined it would be."

"That's for sure," Della muttered. "Well, it sounds like you did okay. Did you take a nap or anything?"

"I tried, but I couldn't sleep," Maia wailed. "I just kept seeing that guy lying in the ravine."

"You need some sleep," Della said. "You'll feel much better. Really. I slept almost all day. And I'm feeling . . ."

"What?"

"I'm feeling better. Really, I am. You know, what happened to that guy last night was an accident."

"I know," Maia said, wiping her running nose with her hand.

"He attacked me. It's not like he was some innocent kid."

"Yes, I know," Maia repeated edgily.

"He fell and he was killed. It's not like I intentionally tried to kill him. It was an accident. You have to remember that. An accident."

"I know."

"Well then, what has you so upset, Maia?" Della asked patiently.

"It's just that . . . we're going to be caught. Everyone's going to find out. About the accident. About us being there by ourselves without Mr. Abner . . . about everything."

"That's just not true," Della insisted. "It'll be weeks or months before the body is discovered—if ever. There won't be anything to tie us to it."

Maia started to cry again. It took Della a long time to calm her down. They talked for more than two hours, with Della doing her best to reassure Maia that all their lives would soon return to normal and that their secret would remain one.

At first she felt angry that Maia was acting so much more upset than she was. After all, Della had been the one who was attacked, the one who shoved him, the one who . . . killed him.

But looking around at the frilly room filled with dolls and stuffed animals, and thinking about Maia's strict, overbearing parents, Della became more understanding. Maia didn't have much of an opportunity to act like a grown-up. Her parents were doing everything they could to keep her a child.

By the time Della had finished talking to her, Maia seemed much calmer. "Now, get some sleep," Della told her, heading toward the bedroom door. "You'll feel much better tomorrow. I know you will."

"Thanks, Della," Maia said, smiling for the first time. "Sorry I'm being such a drag."

Della waved good-night and headed downstairs and out of the house. It felt good to breathe some fresh air. Maia's room had been hot and stuffy. Della was surprised to see the pavement wet. It must have rained while she'd been inside.

She walked quickly along the street, which seemed to glow from the streetlights being reflected on the wet pavement. The wet lawns glowed too, and Della suddenly had the feeling she was walking on a different planet, a green, wet, glowing planet of soft light and eerie silence.

Her house was dark except for the yellow porchlight. Her mother must have gone to bed early. She pulled open the screen door and something dropped at her feet.

An envelope.

She bent down and picked it up. She examined it under the yellow light. There was no writing on the outside of it. Just a black smudge, probably a fingerprint, in the lower right corner.

She felt something bumpy inside.

She let the screen door close and stepped back to open the envelope. She tilted it and let the bumpy object drop into her hand.

It was a tiny silver skull.

A skull from the chain around the dead man's neck?

Peering into the envelope, she saw a small square of note paper inside. Her hand shaking, she pulled it out.

A single line was scrawled in pencil on one side.

It said: I SAW WHAT YOU DID.

chapter
8

"*M*y first thought was that it was one of your tricks, Ricky," Della said, jabbing his flabby chest with her index finger.

Ricky backed away, looking terribly hurt. "Della, give me a break. I wouldn't pull anything that stupid."

"You mean as stupid as hiding the canoes?" Suki chimed in.

They were sitting tensely around Della's living room, everyone from the overnight except for Pete, who'd be late because his family always ate dinner late. It was Tuesday night, two nights after Della had found the skull and note tucked in her door. Her mother was playing bridge at the Garrisons', up the street.

Although they really didn't want to get together, especially so soon after the overnight, the six members of the Outdoors Club realized they had no choice. They couldn't just ignore the envelope.

They had to try to figure out who had put it there—and why.

"Are you sure you didn't do this?" Suki accused Ricky, glaring at him with obvious dislike.

"Cut Ricky some slack," Gary broke in. "He isn't totally insensitive, you know."

"Yes, I am," Ricky said, grinning at Gary. "But I didn't grab the skull off the dead guy's neck and leave it for Della."

"Look," Gary said, standing up and reaching into his jeans pocket. "I got one too." He pulled out an identical silver skull.

"Gary—how? Where'd you get it?" Della asked.

"I went out for the mail after school yesterday afternoon, and it was in the mailbox," Gary said. Suki grabbed the skull out of his hand to examine it.

"Was there a note, too?" Della asked.

"No. No note."

"This is weird," Ricky said.

"He's very deep, isn't he?" Suki cracked.

"Lay off, Suki!" Ricky cried heatedly.

"Make me," Suki muttered. She handed the skull back to Gary.

"Please. We've got to cool it," Gary said, looking at Suki. "We can't start going at each other's throats. We've got a real problem here. Whoever dropped off these skulls knows where we live!"

The room grew silent. Della shuddered, thinking about someone standing on her front porch, opening the screen door and tucking in the envelope. Someone standing right outside her front door. Someone who saw them that night in the ravine.

Someone who watched them cover the man's body with leaves.

And then? And then this someone, this witness to their crime, did what? Uncovered the body? Pulled the silver skulls off the chain? Delivered them to Della and Gary? For what reason?

"Did anybody else get anything?" Ricky asked. "I didn't."

"I didn't either," Suki said.

Maia shook her head no. Sitting in an overstuffed armchair in the corner with her legs tucked tightly beneath her and a frown frozen on her face, she hadn't said a word the entire time.

"Where's Pete?" Suki asked.

"He'll be here soon," Della said. "But he told me this afternoon he didn't get anything."

"Why just us two?" Gary wondered. He got up from where he was sitting beside Suki on the leather couch and walked to the living room window. "Why just us two?"

He stopped suddenly and turned around. "Hey— I just thought of something. I lost my wallet. Did anybody else lose a wallet?"

"I did," Della answered, raising her hand as if she were in school.

No one else said anything.

"It was in my backpack. I'm sure of it," Della said, walking over to Gary at the window.

"Mine too," he said. "Maybe that explains how the guy got our addresses."

Della suddenly remembered the noises she'd heard from the tent late at night, the footsteps she'd followed. Maybe they weren't caused by a raccoon after all. Maybe someone had been there, just a few feet from where she had slept. Maybe this someone had gone through the backpacks and stolen the two wallets.

Della looked out into the dark front yard. He could be out there right now, she thought. She walked quickly to the side of the window and pulled the curtains shut.

"We've got to go to the police," Gary said suddenly, looking at Della.

"No!" Maia cried, her first word of the night. "You can't! I mean, we can't."

"But, Maia—" Gary started.

"We've all got too much to lose. Our parents will never trust us again," Maia shouted, tensely gripping the side of the armchair. "Everyone in town will know that—"

"But this guy knows where we live!" Gary shouted back at her. He tossed the silver skull high in the air. It hit the ceiling and dropped to the beige carpet at Maia's feet.

"Gary, cool your jets," Suki said. She patted the couch cushion beside her. "Come back and sit down. Let's all try to think about this calmly, okay?"

Gary shook his head. "I'm calm," he insisted. But he came back and sat down next to Suki, leaning forward on the couch, putting his hands between his knees and loudly cracking his knuckles.

"Yeah, you're real calm, okay," Suki said. "So what do you think this guy with the skulls wants anyway?"

"I don't know," Gary said, cracking the knuckles of his other hand.

"To frighten us, I guess," Della said.

"But not to turn us in," Suki added. "If he was going to turn us in to the police, he would've done it already, right?"

"Probably," Gary admitted.

"If he was going to report the body, he would've reported it," Suki continued. "But that's not what he wants. He just wants to make us squirm, to frighten us. Why?"

Gary shrugged.

"Just for kicks, right?"

"Maybe."

"Well, what if we don't scare so easy?" Suki suggested. "What if he doesn't frighten us, and we don't go running to the police? What if we just ignore his stupid skulls? He'll probably just go away."

"She's right!" Maia cried, perhaps the first time she had ever agreed with Suki.

"But you're forgetting a few important things," Della interrupted, standing behind the couch. "For one thing, maybe he wants to do more than scare us. Maybe he wants to blackmail us or something. If he really saw what we did, if he really was there in the ravine watching us, he could hold it over us. He could blackmail us, blackmail our parents."

"Yes, but—" Suki started.

"Let me finish," Della insisted, hitting the arm of the couch with her open hand. "Even more important, look what this guy did. He stood by and spied on us. Then he unburied the corpse. Then he robbed it. He stole the dead man's necklace. This guy is a creep, some kind of weirdo. He could do *anything*. We could all be in danger."

"But if he really wanted to hurt us, to do something awful, he already had his chance," Suki argued. "But all he's doing is leaving little skulls around. I don't think that's enough to—"

She was interrupted by a loud knock on the front door.

"That must be Pete," Della said, hurrying across the room. "Hi," she said, pulling open the door.

But no one was there.

"Hey!" Surprised, she opened the screen door and stepped out. She didn't see anyone. She came back inside, pushing the door closed and locking it.

"Am I hearing things?" she asked. "You all heard a knock too, didn't you?"

"Maybe it's him. Maybe he's come back," Maia said, looking very frightened. "Are all the doors locked?"

"I think so," Della said. "I'll go check." She ran to the kitchen to make sure the back door was locked. It was. Then she checked the sliding glass doors in the den. They weren't locked. She struggled to pull down the lock. This door was always difficult, but she managed it.

She looked out through the glass into the dark backyard. A pale sliver of a moon was just climbing over the red garage roof. She pressed her forehead against the cool glass.

What was that shadow moving across the lawn? Had she imagined it? No.

She pulled back from the window and pressed herself against the wall. Carefully, she moved her head forward just enough so that she could see out.

It was just a cat.

She took a deep breath and let it out slowly. Her

heart was pounding. Her hands suddenly felt ice cold.

That was stupid, she thought. Frightening myself over a cat.

She realized the others must be wondering where she was all this time. Checking the back-door lock one more time just to be sure, she headed down the hall.

She was nearly to the living room when she heard the loud knocking on the front door again.

chapter

9

"*W*ho's there?" Della called.

No reply.

Gary joined her in the hallway. "Who is it?" he shouted.

Silence on the other side of the door.

Impulsively, Gary turned the lock and started to pull the knob. "No, Gary—don't!" Della cried. But she was too late. He had already pulled open the door.

There was no one on the front porch.

Gary pushed open the screen door and stepped outside. Down on the street, a car with only one headlight squealed around the corner and sped past, going much faster than the thirty-five mph speed limit. As it passed under a streetlight, Della could see that it was packed with teenagers.

That's what we should be doing, she thought wistfully. Out cruising around, having a good time.

"Gary—please. Come back in," Della called,

watching him through the screen door as he explored the front yard.

"No one out here," he said, sounding relieved. He stepped back onto the porch. "The ground is soft, but I don't see any footprints." He scratched his head of wavy blond hair.

"Maybe it's a ghost," Della joked.

"Someone's playing a little joke," Gary said, reentering the house and walking past her in the hallway. "An unfunny joke."

Della closed the door and carefully locked it. They walked back into the living room.

Ricky, Maia, and Suki were standing tensely by the window. "Is he—is he out there?" Maia asked.

Gary shrugged. "I didn't see anyone."

"But who's knocking?" Maia demanded, clenching her hands into tight fists at her sides.

"The Ghost of Christmas Past," Della said.

No one laughed.

"Maybe we *should* go to the cops," Suki said, looking worried for the first time. She was wearing an oversized turquoise sweater that came down nearly to her knees. She wrapped her arms around herself, nearly disappearing into the voluminous sweater.

"No!" Maia insisted. "We still have no reason to. It may be some neighborhood kid playing a stupid prank on us."

"I used to play this joke," Ricky admitted, smiling.

"Big surprise," Suki said sarcastically.

"I used to think it was pretty funny," Ricky said. He walked over to the couch and stretched out, laying his head on the soft arm cushion. "Now I'm not so sure."

"We're sitting ducks here," Della said glumly.

"Look, let's not go over the edge," Gary told her. "The guy's just playing a joke. If he wanted to get in or do something really terrible, he had two chances when the door was open. He just wants to make us squirm."

"We're squirming," Ricky said. "We're squirming!"

"Let's be ready for him the next time he knocks," Gary said.

"What are you talking about, Gary?" Della asked warily. Gary was a great guy and everyone liked him. But one reason why people liked him so much was that he wasn't perfect—sometimes he did crazy, foolhardy things, things that kids would talk about for weeks afterward.

Della knew Gary really well. She had gone out with him for a long time, after all. And she knew the look on Gary's face. It was a look she wasn't happy to see. It was his *daring* look. It was his fixed expression of *daring* anyone to stop what he was about to do next.

"Come on, Gary. What are you thinking?" Della demanded, following him across the living room.

"Nothing much. Don't look at me like that, Della. I'm not going to do anything crazy. I just want to get a look at this joker."

"Let's just go home," Maia said, joining them in the hallway. Ricky and Suki nervously followed her.

"But the party's just starting!" Ricky exclaimed, and then laughed as if he'd made a hilarious joke.

"Come on, Maia. We've got to wait for Pete," Della said.

"And besides, we haven't settled anything," Suki added. "We haven't decided what to do about the skulls and the note."

"Do? What can we do?" Maia whined. "One thing we can do is not sit around this house and let that creep terrorize us."

Gary had disappeared up the stairs. Now he returned carrying Della's Polaroid camera in his hands. "How about a group portrait?" he asked, smiling.

"That's the only way you'll ever get this group to smile," Ricky cracked.

"Here's another way you can get me to smile, Schorr—leave!" Suki scowled.

"Knock it off, Suki," Gary warned. "Stop picking on Ricky."

"Ricky's picking on *me* by existing," Suki muttered.

"Remind me to laugh at that one later," Ricky said, rolling his eyes.

"Come on, you two," Della pleaded.

"I'm going. Really. I have to go home," Maia said, pushing past them to the door.

"No! Don't!" Gary said, pulling her back. "You'll chase him away before I can get his picture."

"That's your plan?" Della cried. "When he knocks, you're going to pull open the door, yell 'Smile!' and take his picture?"

"Yeah," Gary said defensively. "That's my plan. You got a better one?"

"Yeah. Forget it."

"What if he doesn't want his picture taken?" Suki asked.

"What if it makes him mad?" Ricky asked.

"Let me go home—please!" Maia begged.

"After I flash the picture, Della, slam the door and lock it. He'll be too stunned to react quickly," Gary said. "Then we'll call the police." He looked at Della. "What do you think?"

Della rolled her eyes to the ceiling. "Dumb," she said. "But I can see that you're going to do it anyway."

Gary smiled. "Right."

"Please—let me go," Maia repeated.

"Maia, stop. We're all in this together. We have to stick together. We have to help each other," Della said.

"Then let's *all* leave!" Ricky said. He quickly held up both hands. "A joke. Just a joke!"

Maia scowled and angrily walked back to the living room. "You can't keep me a prisoner here," she called.

"You're not a prisoner," Suki said. "But you can't be a deserter either."

"But you're all acting crazy!" Maia insisted, her voice high and tense. "I just want this all to be over."

"That's what we all want," Suki said. "But running home to Mommy won't do that, Maia."

"Ssh. We've got to be ready," Gary said, ignoring her and positioning the camera. "The instant he knocks, Della, pull open the door. You've got to be fast or we'll miss him."

"But how—" Della started to say.

But before she could finish her question, they all heard a loud knock on the door.

Della jumped in astonishment. Time seemed to freeze.

Her breath seemed to freeze.

Everyone in the hallway seemed to freeze.

The knock was repeated.

Somehow she got herself breathing again. Somehow she got her brain to work, her arm to move. Somehow she turned the lock and, with one swift motion, pulled the door open wide.

Gary stepped forward and clicked the camera. The flash sent a burst of white light through the hallway and out onto the porch.

chapter

10

*T*he flash of light revealed movement, a face, a blur of hair, dark clothes. It was a man. He disappeared as quickly as the light.

He leaped off the side of the porch. Della heard him hit the bushes and keep moving.

He must be around the side of the house by now, she thought.

The surprise of it, the fact that some stranger really was on the porch, froze both Della and Gary. It was almost as if *they* had been caught by the camera and frozen on film.

By the time they pushed open the screen door and peered out, there was no sign of anyone.

"The film. The picture. Look. It's developing." Gary's hand was trembling as he held the Polaroid picture and watched the colors darken.

Maia, Suki, and Ricky were standing behind them now. All of them stared in silence as the picture sharpened and filled in.

"Nice shot of the screen door," Ricky said, shaking his head.

The screen door looked shiny and silvery in the photo. Beyond it was only darkness, not even the blur of the man moving off the porch.

"We didn't get him," Della said.

"Back to the drawing board," Gary muttered, disappointed.

Someone stepped suddenly onto the porch.

Oh no! We didn't close the door! Della thought. He's circled the house and come back!

She grabbed the door and started to slam it.

"Hey—what's the big idea?!" the shadowy figure on the porch screamed.

"Pete!" everyone cried, very relieved.

Pete looked confused. "Sorry I'm late. Nice of you to all come to the door to greet me. I see the party's going full swing."

"It hasn't been much of a party," Della said with a sigh. "We've had a visitor." She reached past him to lock the door. "Did you see anyone out there?"

"No. No one." Pete stared at the camera. "Taking pictures?"

"Yeah. We're starting a family album," Ricky quipped.

"Count me out. I don't want Schorr in *my* family!" Suki said.

Maia headed back into the living room and slumped down in the armchair, looking more glum than ever. "Can I go now?" she groaned.

"Guess it isn't much of a party," Pete agreed as the rest of them trooped after her.

Maia made a face. "I'm leaving," she said. But she made no attempt to get up from the chair.

"Wait, Maia," Pete said. "I brought something. I think you'll want to see it."

He pulled a folded-up newspaper clipping out of the pocket of his chinos and spread it out on the coffee table. Everyone gathered around to look at it.

It was from the Shadyside *Beacon*. The headline read:

NEIGHBORS WITNESS BURGLARY, FATAL SHOOTING

A smaller headline underneath read:

POLICE HUNT TWO MEN IN KILLING

"Read it out loud," Suki said to Pete.

"That's because she can't read," Ricky cracked. Suki gave him a hard poke in the stomach with her elbow.

"You read it, Della," Pete said, handing the clipping to her. "I still have a big, flashing light in my eyes."

The news story reported that neighbors had seen two young men break into a local gardener's home. There were gunshots, the witnesses said, then the two men ran out of the house, empty-handed.

The gardener was found shot dead inside his house. Rumored to be an eccentric millionaire, he had supposedly hidden a fortune in cash in his small cottage—the goal of the intruders, police guessed. When the burglars didn't find the money, the police continued, they must have attacked the gardener and killed him.

The two men were still at large, the article concluded, and finding them was the number-one priority of the police. A neighbor had gotten a good look as they fled. The police sketch of the burglar was beside the article.

"Oh no! Look at the face!" Della cried, holding the clipping up so everyone could see it.

It was the man on Fear Island, the man she had buried in the ravine.

"So he was a killer," Suki said, taking the clipping, staring at the sketch as if memorizing it, then passing it back to Della. "So we don't have to feel so bad."

"He said something to me about an old man," Della said, suddenly remembering. "He started talking really fast, really crazy, and he said something about not being able to communicate with an old man, having to teach him a lesson or something. It didn't make any sense at the time. I was so frightened, I really couldn't hear what he was saying."

"Well, now we know who he is," Pete said, folding up the clipping and shoving it back into his pocket, "and we know who watched us bury him in the leaves. And we know who left the silver skull for Della. It's his partner."

His partner.

So that was the explanation, Della thought. The young man wasn't alone in the woods. He and his partner must have been hiding out there. Who would think of looking for them on that uninhabited island?

And the partner had been hiding in the woods on the edge of the ravine. The partner saw everything.

"What do you think this guy wants?" Maia asked softly.

They had all become very quiet as they thought about the news Pete had brought. They realized their secret was not entirely secret anymore. Someone else was in on it, someone who had murdered an old man. Someone who knew where Gary and Della lived. Someone who had been right outside the door.

"He obviously doesn't want to thank us," Suki said dryly.

"Maybe he wants revenge," Ricky suggested.

Everyone looked at Ricky, as if to make sure he was serious. He was.

A feeling of gloom settled over the room. No one said anything for a while.

"Which is worse—having him want to blackmail us or having him want revenge?" Gary asked, breaking the silence.

"How could he blackmail us?" Maia asked. Her face was red. She looked as if she were about to start crying.

"Not us. Our parents," Pete said, looking at the floor. "They didn't get anything from that robbery. The partner probably sees us as a way to cash in."

"Most of our parents are pretty well off," Gary said.

"Speak for yourself. Mine don't have a dime," Suki snapped with some bitterness.

Gary ignored her. "This partner could tell our parents everything. He could threaten to expose us to the police if our parents don't come up with big money."

"No! That's impossible! That's *horrible!*" Maia cried.

"Whoa. Hold it a minute," Della said, jumping up from the piano bench where she'd been thinking about all this in silence. "That doesn't make any sense at all."

"Nothing makes sense," Suki muttered.

"This partner—he can't go to the police. He killed an old man, remember?" Della said.

"Della's right," Maia broke in, sounding a little relieved.

"He can't go walking into the police station and tell the cops he saw us kill his partner."

"The police would probably thank us, anyway," Ricky said, brightening. "They'd probably give us a reward or something."

"That's not true," Della said, shaking her head impatiently. "But there's no way the partner is going to the police."

"He could threaten to tip off the police. It would be easy for him just to phone them and tell them what he saw," Pete said.

"He's right," Maia cried, horrified.

"So take your pick," Della said mournfully. "Blackmail or revenge?"

"We're dead meat either way," Suki said glumly. "He could blackmail us for the rest of our lives."

"We'd better call the police," Gary said firmly.

"The police won't be able to protect you and Della," Maia argued.

"Oh, Maia—stop thinking about yourself for once!" Della exploded, finally losing her patience.

"You're only worried about your parents finding out that you went on the overnight without a chaperone. You don't care *what* happens to the rest of us!"

Maia's mouth dropped open and her face turned as red as a tomato. Della immediately regretted blowing up at her friend. Now she'd be spending months apologizing to her. And what had she accomplished by yelling like that? Nothing at all. She wasn't going to change Maia.

"That's not true!" Maia protested. "I just . . . I just . . . Okay. I won't say another word." She crossed her arms defiantly in front of her and glared furiously at Della.

"But Maia's right," Pete said suddenly, looking at Della. "What are the police going to do to protect you—to protect any of us—from this creep? Nothing. Are they going to put a full-time guard around your house? Or escort you to school and back? No way."

"With our help, the police might be able to catch the partner," Della said.

"When?" Ricky broke in. "After we're all murdered in our sleep?"

"Stop it! Don't *say* that!" Maia screamed.

"Please—we're all getting hysterical," Suki said. "We've got to chill out. So far, all the guy has done is—"

She stopped when she heard the knock on the front door.

They all froze. Maia let out a little cry and sank deep into the armchair. Della looked to the front door as if waiting for someone to come bursting in.

"I, I left the camera on the stairway," Gary said in a loud whisper.

"I'm not going to answer it," Della whispered. "I don't think we should answer it."

No one agreed or disagreed. They were all staring toward the front hallway in frightened silence.

Another knock, this time longer and louder.

"Why is he *doing* this?" Maia cried.

"Come on, let's answer it," Gary said, moving toward the door. "There won't be anyone there anyway."

"No, Gary—" Della started.

But he had made up his mind. He jogged to the front entrance, hesitated for a second, then put his face close to the door and yelled, "Who is it?"

There was a brief silence. And then a man on the other side of the door said, "We're back!"

chapter

11

Gary looked confused for a second. Then he turned the lock and pulled open the front door.

Della's mother and a tall, bald man walked in.

"Oh, hi, Gary. What a nice surprise," Mrs. O'Connor said, looking a bit startled. "This is Mr. Garrison. He walked me home."

"Your mother forgot her house key," Mr. Garrison explained to Della.

Mrs. O'Connor poked her head into the living room and was further startled to see that Della had even more visitors. "Della—a party on a school night?"

Some party, Della thought. "What are *you* doing here?" she blurted out. "I mean, why are you back so early?"

"No one was much in the mood for bridge tonight. So we decided to break up early," Mrs. O'Connor said. "What's going on here?" she asked, tossing her pocketbook down on a side table and striding into the center of the room.

"Mom, I'd like you to meet the members of the Outdoors Club," Della said, regaining her composure. She introduced everyone to her mother.

"I like your hair," Mrs. O'Connor said to Suki. "How do you get it to stand up like that?"

"I use a gel," Suki said, trying to figure out if Della's mom was putting her on or not.

"It's very . . . what do they call it? Very . . . rad," Mrs. O'Connor said.

Ricky started to laugh, then quickly stopped.

"No, I really do like it," Mrs. O'Connor insisted. "Of course, if Della did that to her hair, I'd murder her!"

"Mom, please . . ." Della interrupted.

"And why the special club meeting?" Mrs. O'Connor asked, ignoring her daughter's protest.

"Oh . . . we were just talking about the overnight," Della answered, thinking quickly.

"I hear it was a great success," Mrs. O'Connor said, straightening a pile of magazines on the coffee table. She never could just stand and talk. She always had to be doing something useful at the same time.

"Oh, yes. Great," Gary said.

"It was rad," Ricky added. No one laughed. If Mrs. O'Connor realized that he was making fun of her, she didn't let on.

"We were just finishing, actually," Della said, looking at the others to make sure they understood it was time to leave.

"Yes. Meeting adjourned," Gary said. He smiled

at Mrs. O'Connor. "I'm the president. If I didn't say that, they couldn't go home."

Della's mother laughed her high-pitched laugh. "It's so nice to see you, Gary," she said. "We've missed you around here."

Gary turned bright red and looked very embarrassed. Della would have enjoyed his discomfort, except that she felt equally embarrassed.

Everyone said good-bye and walked out into the night, except for Pete, who lingered uncomfortably in the doorway. "Uh . . . Della . . . can I talk to you for a minute?"

"Sure," Della said, wondering why he looked so nervous. Was he afraid to go outside because the dead man's partner might be lurking out there? No. She hoped he didn't want to talk more about the partner and everything else, not with her mom so near.

"I was wondering . . ." he said, leading her out onto the front porch for privacy, "if maybe . . . you'd like to go out with me Friday night?"

"Oh." It wasn't at all what she had expected. She took a deep breath. The air felt cool and sweet. She could smell the apple blossoms from the tree across the driveway. "Yes. Okay." She smiled at him. "Sounds okay."

He smiled back. "I'll pick you up after eight, okay? Maybe we'll go to a movie. Or maybe to The Mill."

"Fine."

The ancient, collapsing mill, built at the end of Old Mill Road before the town of Shadyside even existed, had recently been resurrected and reopened as a teen dance club called The Mill. A lot of Della's friends from Shadyside High went there just about every weekend to dance and meet guys. But she had a hard time picturing Pete there in his crisply pleated chinos and Ralph Lauren polo shirts.

Maybe he isn't such a stiff after all, she thought, watching him head down the driveway to his station wagon. He's been so sweet to me. Maybe he's just what I need to help me forget about Gary.

She shivered suddenly, remembering that someone might be out there. Someone might be hiding in the darkness, staring at her, watching her right now, plotting against her, hating her.

Still shivering, she turned and bolted into the house, slamming the door loudly behind her, so loudly that dogs began barking and howling all down the block.

"I can't believe I'm having such a great time!" Della said to herself. It was Friday night, and she and Pete had already been dancing at The Mill for more than an hour. She laughed and slapped him playfully on the shoulder as he attempted a ridiculous dance maneuver on one leg.

Actually, Pete wasn't a good dancer. In fact, he had no sense of rhythm at all. But at least he tried. He even made jokes about his dancing. I never even knew he had a sense of humor, Della thought, scolding herself for having such a wrong impression of him.

The club was hot and crowded. Teenagers packed the dance floor, bumping into each other as they moved to the deafening music, the insistent drums pounding out a steady rhythm through the massive speakers suspended in every corner of the huge room. Swirling blue and magenta lights made it seem as if the floor were spinning. Crowds of kids watched the dancers from the refreshment bar that ran the entire length of the building, or from the low balcony that overhung the dance floor.

Della and Pete danced nonstop. It was far too noisy to talk. A little after midnight she pulled him out into the parking lot. "Enough! I'm totally wrecked!" she cried happily.

He laughed. Even though it was a warm night, the air felt cool against their hot faces. When she looked up at the sky, Della could still see the swirling colors of the lights. The pounding rhythm floated out from the dance club, drums and bass guitar driving to the same beat as her heart.

"Want to get something to eat?" he asked.

"I don't know. It's so late." She knew she should be tired, but she felt just the opposite, keyed up, eager to keep moving, totally wired.

"Let's go get a hamburger," he said, pulling her by the hand. His own hand was hot and wet.

She pulled back suddenly, catching him off guard, and he stumbled close. Impulsively, she reached her hand up behind his neck, held him, and gave him a long kiss.

When she backed away, he looked stunned.

"That was a good-night kiss," she said, laughing at his shocked expression. "I just wanted to get it over with. Now let's go get a hamburger."

They climbed into the front of the station wagon and immediately rolled down the windows, trying to cool off. Pete backed out of the parking space and headed out of the still-crowded parking lot.

Another car, its brights on, followed close behind. Pete pulled out onto Old Mill Road, squinting into the mirror. "Wish he'd turn his brights off," he muttered.

The road was empty, nothing but darkness up ahead as far as Della could see. There wasn't much reason to drive on this far edge of town so late at night unless you were on the way to or from The Mill.

Della settled back into the seat, resting her knees against the dashboard. She felt great, relaxed and happily tired. But she could see that something was troubling Pete. "What's wrong?"

"This guy won't get off my tail," Pete complained, looking into the rearview mirror.

"Slow down. Maybe he'll go around," she suggested.

Pete slowed down. Della turned around to look out the back window. The car behind didn't pass them. Instead, it slowed down too.

"Maybe it's someone we know," Della suggested. "I can't tell. The bright lights are blinding me." The back window was filled with light, so it was impossible to see anything through it.

Pete slowed down even more. Then he pulled to the side of the road onto the soft dirt shoulder. "Hey, what's the big idea?" he shouted out the window.

The other car pulled over too, and stopped just inches behind them. Pete reached for the door handle, to climb out. "No, wait," Della said, grabbing his other arm. She suddenly felt fearful.

What if this wasn't someone they knew? What if this was . . . someone they *didn't* want to know?

She hadn't thought about the dead man and his partner all night. But now the whole thing flashed once again through her mind.

"Don't get out, Pete. Lock your door."

He gave her a funny look, but followed her advice.

They watched the car behind them, he through the rearview mirror, she through the back window, waiting for someone to open the door, to step out so they could see him or her.

But the door didn't open. Whoever it was in the car behind them gunned the engine until it roared.

"I'm scared," Della admitted. "Let's get out of here, Pete."

Obligingly, he put the car into drive and floored the gas pedal. The tires spun loudly on the soft ground and the car lurched back onto the road. Pete lost control for a moment as it skidded onto the pavement. Then he quickly guided it back into the lane and, keeping his foot down hard, sped away.

Della sank back onto the seat, trying to force herself not to panic. She looked over at the glowing green speedometer. They were doing 85.

"Please," Della said aloud without realizing it. "Please go away, whoever you are."

They heard a squeal behind them, followed by the roar of the other car's engine. Bright yellow lights reflected off the rearview mirror again, filling the car with light and fast-moving shadows.

"I don't believe this!" Pete cried. The wheel was bouncing in his hand. It was taking all of his skill and concentration to steer along the curving old road at such a high speed. "He's still on our tail! This is crazy!"

He pressed harder on the gas pedal. Della saw the needle go up to 90.

"What are we doing?" she cried. "This is insane! I hate car chases in the movies! I never expected to be in one in real life!"

"Check your seat belt," Pete said. "Sometimes that one slides loose."

"Oh, thanks for telling me!" she cried. "You picked a fine time to mention it!"

Pete looked into the mirror, and his expression became more worried. "He—He's speeding up!"

"But he's right behind us. He'll crash into us!" Della screamed, ducking down low and closing her eyes.

"My dad'll kill me," Pete said. "He loves this wagon."

"How can you worry about the car?" Della shouted over the roar of the engine. "What about your life!"

"You don't know my dad," Pete said, veering into the left lane, then swerving back into the right. "He really cares about his possessions."

"Oh!" Della cried, as she felt the impact, then another bumpbumpbump, as the car behind them banged into their rear bumper.

"What the—" Pete's eyes stared straight ahead as he struggled to keep control of the car. "Is he really trying to ram us off the road . . . or is it just a game, or what?"

Della shut her eyes tight and gripped the sides of the bucket seat. She cried out again as they were bumped hard from behind, the car seeming to bounce up off the road and then come down with its tires spinning.

"Turn off!" she cried. "Turn onto another road. Maybe he won't follow."

"I can't turn," Pete said, his voice revealing his fright. "I'm going too fast. I don't know if I can keep control."

They were bumped again, this time even harder. The bright lights seemed to circle the car, infiltrating every corner, surrounding them in a harsh yellow glare.

"It's a Taurus," Pete said, his eyes on the mirror. "Know anybody who has a black Taurus?"

"No," Della said. "What are we going to do?"

"Hold on tight," Pete said. "This may be stupid, but I'm going to try it. If it doesn't work . . . well . . . it's been real."

"What are you going to do?" she asked.

But instead of answering, he slammed his foot on the brake and spun the wheel. The car squealed and slid for about a hundred yards, then spun around. The other car veered wildly to the right to get out of the way, then roared past.

Pete frantically moved the wheel, trying to bring the wagon out of its spin. They had completely turned around now and were facing the way they had come. He floored the gas pedal again and they moved forward.

"That's an old Kojak trick!" Pete exclaimed, obviously relieved that he was still alive to tell her that. "You okay?"

"I don't know. I guess. Did we lose him?"

Pete looked into the mirror. "Yeah. I think so. We—"

They heard the squeal of brakes and tires.

"He's turning around!"

Then they heard a crash, so loud Pete's hands flew up in the air. Della screamed but couldn't hear herself.

The crash was followed by a hideous crunching sound, the sound of glass shattering and metal hitting wood.

Pete eased the wagon to a stop. Della's heart was pounding. At first she had thought *they* had crashed! It was all so unreal. It took a long time for her to realize that the other car had slid off the road and smacked into the trees.

"We've got to go back," Pete said. "Whoever it is has got to be in bad shape after that."

"I guess," Della said with a shudder. She turned to Pete. "Are you okay?"

"Yeah," he said, turning the wagon around. "I'm okay. This is a pretty exciting first date, don't you think?"

"Shut up," she said teasingly.

He eased the car around and drove slowly back until they saw the Taurus. Its headlights were still on but they were shining up toward the sky. The car was tilted against a massive tree trunk. With its tires still spinning, it looked as if it were trying to climb the tree.

As they drove closer, Pete and Della saw that the right side of the car was completely smashed in. Surprisingly, the driver's side was relatively unharmed. Shards of glass lay scattered across the road.

"Let's go see how bad he's hurt," Pete said.

Della grasped his arm tightly but didn't move.

"You don't want to come with me?" he asked

softly. "That's okay. No problem. You can stay in the car."

"No," she said, suddenly feeling a wave of nausea. "No. I want to get out of the car. I want to see who it is in there, who was doing that to us."

Pete opened his door and stepped out. He walked around the front of the station wagon and opened the passenger door for her.

Della climbed out unsteadily and they made their way, following the beam of their headlights, to the driver's side of the wrecked car.

"Now let's see exactly who it is," Della said. She gripped the handle and pulled open the door to the Taurus.

The car was empty.

chapter

12

"*S*o who was it in the car?" Maia asked. "Who was chasing you?"

"I don't know," Della told her with a shrug.

It was Monday afternoon, and they were leaning against the yellow tile wall just outside the door to Mr. Abner's room. School had let out ten minutes earlier and already the halls were nearly deserted.

Della had just told the whole frightening story about the Friday-night car chase to Maia, the first person from the Outdoors Club she had seen. She was reluctant to talk about it, but she just *had* to tell someone. Now she regretted it because Maia looked pale and shaky.

"You don't know who was in the car?" Maia asked, not understanding.

"There was *no one* in the car," Della explained, whispering even though the corridor was empty.

"You mean—"

"Whoever it was must have run off into the woods before we got to the car."

"That's so scary," Maia said, pressing the back of her head against the wall and closing her eyes. "Do you think it was—"

"The partner? Maybe," Della said. "It wasn't a kid from school or anything. No one we know would try such a dangerous stunt."

"But why would he—" Maia started. She stopped when Ricky bounced up beside them.

"Talking about me again, huh?" he said, putting his chubby arms around them both. "Well, I'm sorry. You both can't have me. You'll have to fight it out among yourselves."

He laughed and walked past them into the classroom. Maia frowned with disgust. They could hear him greeting Suki, Gary, and Pete.

"He's not so bad," Della said.

"Not so bad as what? Not so bad as bubonic plague?" Maia exclaimed. Then her face filled with concern. "So are you okay? You weren't hurt or anything?"

"No," Della assured her. "Pete and I were okay. Just a little scared. We drove home *very* slowly." She swung her bookbag from one hand to the other and shifted her weight. "I haven't been able to sleep too well, though. Every time I fall asleep, I see headlights and I dream I'm being chased again."

"That's awful," Maia said, shaking her head sadly. "I've been having bad dreams too. What a mistake we all made. If only we'd stayed home instead of . . . Uh-oh. Here comes Mr. Abner."

"Hi, girls. Sorry I'm late," he called to them from down the hall. He strode quickly up to them, his brown leather cowboy boots clicking loudly on the floor as he walked. With his straight-legged jeans and red-and-black-checked flannel shirt, he looked more like a tall, lanky cowboy than a teacher. All he needed was a bandana around his neck, Della decided.

"What are you two talking about so seriously?" he asked.

"Nothing much," Maia said quickly, blushing.

"Did we look serious?" Della asked teasingly. "That must be a first, right?"

He followed them into the room. They took their seats in the first row. Pete smiled across at Della. Suki was playfully slapping Gary's hand.

Mr. Abner lowered a window blind, blocking the bright sunshine that had been flooding over his desk. "Nice day," he said to no one in particular. "Too bad we were in here and missed it."

"I didn't want to miss it," Ricky said. "So I cut my morning classes!" He laughed loudly so Mr. Abner would know it was a joke.

Mr. Abner gave him a weak smile. Then he sat down on the front of his desk, crossing his legs and looking down at his cowboy boots. "I'm back," he said. "Let me apologize again for having to postpone the overnight. I know you had all worked very hard getting ready for it, and I know how much you were looking forward to it."

Della shifted uncomfortably in her seat. She pulled at a long strand of her dark hair, a nervous habit. She'd been doing it a lot lately, she realized. She had a lot to be nervous about.

Now she was worried that somehow one of them was going to give away the fact that they had gone on the overnight without Mr. Abner. If only he would change the subject, she thought. This is just too dangerous. Of course, no one would deliberately reveal anything. But what if one of them should make a slip. . . .

". . . these family problems. I'm sure you know what I mean," Mr. Abner was saying. Della realized she had missed the whole story he had been telling.

The teacher uncrossed his long legs and recrossed them the other way. "Anyway, I'm back," he said, smiling, "and I have very good news for you."

Everyone was listening very intently now.

"I've been able to reschedule our Fear Island overnight for this coming Saturday," Mr. Abner said. He leaned forward expectantly, awaiting their pleased reaction to his announcement. His smile quickly faded when no one said anything.

"Oh. That's great!" Della exclaimed finally, hoping she sounded just a little bit genuine.

With all of the terror they had experienced in the past two weeks, everyone had forgotten that Mr. Abner would be eager to reschedule the overnight.

"Yeah. Terrific," Ricky said, not being the least bit convincing.

"This weekend? Gosh, I don't know if I can make it," Maia said. "My family is going upstate, I think. To visit . . . uh . . . relatives."

"Yeah. Mine too," Gary said. "I mean . . . not upstate. But I'm pretty sure we have plans, Mr. Abner."

Their advisor looked hurt. "I knew you guys were disappointed before. So I pushed aside some plans of my own." He looked toward the window but couldn't see out because he had closed the blinds. "I have to admit I'm a little surprised by your reaction," he said, scratching his left cheek with his fingernails. "Or rather, your lack of reaction. This *is* the Outdoors Club, right? And you guys have been after me all winter to organize an overnight, right?"

"We're still excited about it," Gary said. "Really."

"I've still got all my gear packed and ready," Della added.

Come on, everyone, she thought. Show a little enthusiasm. Mr. Abner is becoming suspicious. We can't let him start to ask questions about why none of us want to go back to Fear Island. We just can't.

"I'm still crazy to go," said Suki, who had been silent and pensive the whole time. "But I've got to check and see what the plans are for the weekend too." She looked at Gary, as if expecting him to back her up or say something to help.

Gary looked back at her uncomfortably. Then he turned to Mr. Abner and said, "Maybe the club should meet again later in the week. You know, on Wednesday or something. Then we'd all know if we're free or not."

"Well, I guess we'd better," Mr. Abner said, not hiding his disappointment. "I must say, I'm underwhelmed by your enthusiastic response. Is there something going on here that I don't know about?"

A cold chill ran down Della's back. She looked over at Maia, who was tightly gripping the sides of her chair and staring down at the floor.

"I think it's just spring fever," Gary said, grinning reassuringly at Mr. Abner.

"We're all just wrecked from the weekend. I know I did a lot of partying. Too much partying," Suki said.

Everyone laughed uncomfortably.

"We're still looking forward to it," Pete said.

We're looking forward to it like a math test, Della thought. There's no way any of us are ever going back to Fear Island. If only we could level with him. He's not a bad guy. But he's still a teacher. There's no way we can explain anything to him.

"Okay then," Mr. Abner said with a resigned shrug. He stood up quickly. "We're agreed. We'll meet again after school on Wednesday, and you'll let me know if you can fit the overnight into your busy schedules."

He stood up, gathered some papers from his desk, and strode quickly out of the room.

As soon as they were sure he was gone, Gary jumped up, walked to the front of the room and motioned for everyone to stay in their seats. "We've got to talk," he said, nervously looking toward the door. "What are we going to tell Abner?"

"Yeah. How are we getting out of this stupid overnight?" Suki asked, sounding angry for some reason. "There's no way I'm ever camping out again, that's for sure."

"Right on!" Ricky shouted.

Gary motioned for him to lower his voice. "I'm sure we all feel the same way," he said. "So we have to figure out—"

There was a noise out in the hallway, the sound of someone opening a locker.

"We'd better not talk here," Della said.

"Let's go down behind the parking lot," Gary suggested.

"I only have a few minutes," Maia said, looking at her watch. "I told my mom I'd be home at four."

They hurried out the side door and then circled around to the student parking lot behind the building. There were only two cars on the lot. Everyone else had gone home. On the practice field behind the tennis courts, members of the Shadyside baseball team were doing warm-up calisthenics.

"We just have to stall him," Pete suggested as they leaned against the tall metal fence that separated the parking lot from the practice field. "School's out in four or five weeks. If we're all busy on weekends, the overnight just won't take place."

"Maybe we should explain what happened, tell the whole story to Abner," Gary suggested. "It would be good, I think, to tell it to an adult. He wouldn't go to the police or anything. I don't think."

"No!" Maia protested immediately. "It's our secret. We have to keep it our secret. We took a vow, remember?"

The others all quickly agreed with her. There was no telling what Mr. Abner would do if he found out what they had done.

"We can stall him," Suki said with certainty. "We just have to make sure that our stories—"

"Hey, I just remembered something," Ricky interrupted. He turned to Della and poked her on the shoulder with his finger. "My ZAP gun. I came back from the overnight with only five ZAP guns.

You never gave yours back to me. Can you bring it over to my house tonight?''

"Oh no," Della gasped, grabbing the fence. She suddenly felt cold all over.

"Not tonight? Well, can you bring it to school tomorrow?" Ricky asked, not noticing her horrified expression.

"I—I left it," Della managed to say.

"What?"

"I had the gun in the ravine. Then the man . . . he . . . he took it from me and . . ." She shook her head hard as if trying to shake away what she was remembering. She stared at Ricky. "I left the gun with the body. On Fear Island."

"No! That's impossible!" Ricky cried. He slammed his fist against the fence, making it clang. Several of the baseball players looked over at them.

"Shhh. Lower your voice, Ricky," Gary warned.

"But my gun! I mean, you can't leave it there!" he screamed at Della, ignoring Gary. "When the police find the body in the leaves, my gun will be there."

"They won't know it's yours, Schorr," Suki told him with a look of disgust.

"*Everyone* knows I'm into ZAP wars," Ricky said heatedly, turning away from Della and shouting in Suki's face. "Everyone knows I'm the one in school with all the ZAP guns. All the cops have to do is ask any kid at Shadyside who has ZAP guns, and they'll be coming right to me. That gun will lead them right to Ricky Schorr! And I'll tell you one thing—"

Gary pulled him back away from Suki. "Cool your jets, man. Come on, Ricky."

Ricky pulled out of Gary's grasp. "I'll tell you one thing, I'm not taking the blame for that dead guy. If the police come to me, I'm telling them about all of you too."

"You dirty—" Suki's eyes grew wide with hatred.

Gary quickly stepped between them.

"Wait! Stop! Everybody—stop!" Della screamed. They turned to her. "Ricky's right. This is my responsibility. All of it."

"Now wait, Della—" Pete started, but she reached up and put a hand over his mouth to quiet him.

"The gun was my responsibility, and I left it there. So I guess I have no choice. I'll go back . . . back to Fear Island . . . and get your gun for you, Ricky."

"Well, okay," Ricky said, still glaring at Suki.

"Whoa! Hold on!" Pete cried. "You can't go back there alone, Della. I'll go with you."

"Thanks," Della said softly, smiling at him.

"Maybe we should all go," Gary said suddenly.

"What?" Maia cried, looking very upset.

"Yeah. Maybe we should go on the overnight. Then Della could slip away and get the gun back. We're all in this together, after all."

"And if we all go, it won't be so bad," Pete added.

"Well . . . I guess . . ." Suki said, thinking it over. "I guess if anything bad happened this time, Abner would be there. He could stomp on any stranger with those baaad cowboy boots of his."

Everyone laughed. Except Maia.

"But—But what do we do if the partner is

there?'' Maia asked, holding onto the fence and looking down at the ground.

''I hope he is,'' Gary said, his face hardening with anger. ''I'm fed up with all this stupid partner business. I'd like to pound the guy. I really would.''

Della looked doubtful. She hated it when Gary started talking tough. ''You guys really don't have to come,'' she said, her voice shaky.

''We're in this together,'' Gary said. ''Of course we'll come. Right, guys?''

The others, except for Maia, murmured their agreement. Finally Maia said, ''Well, maybe. I guess . . . It couldn't be any worse than the last overnight—could it?''

chapter

13

*A*s they set off across the lake in three canoes—Mr. Abner and the equipment in one canoe, three club members in each of the other two—the weather was not promising. High clouds had drifted across the sun, and both the sky and water were an ominous gray. A light fog made it hard to see where the water left off and the sky began.

No one said anything. Only the sound of the paddles splashing rhythmically in the water and the raucous honking of two large ducks flying overhead broke the silence.

Della leaned forward, looking past Maia to Pete in the front of the canoe, matching her paddle strokes with his. The waves were stronger this trip, tossed by a warm but gusting wind, and it was more difficult to keep the small canoe moving forward.

"Is this a silent movie, or what?" Mr. Abner called from his canoe, several feet ahead of them. "How about some noise, you guys? Anybody know any songs?"

"No!" Ricky, Gary, and Suki called in unison.

"It's too early on a Saturday morning for songs," Suki added.

"Anybody ever tell you guys you're a lot of laughs?" their advisor asked, paddling harder against the current.

"No," Gary called. "Nobody."

"Well, they were right!" Mr. Abner retorted.

Everyone offered him a half-hearted laugh.

"I can't believe we're doing this," Maia muttered. "I can't believe we're going back to that dreadful island."

"Maia—shhh," Della warned. "The wind could carry your voice. You know why we have to go back. Let's just try to make the best of it."

Maia frowned, closed her eyes and slipped her hands under her sweatshirt to warm them.

A light drizzle began to fall. The gray sky grew darker. The thickening fog made everything seem eerie and menacing.

Perfect, Della thought. This is just the perfect atmosphere for a return to Fear Island, a return to the scene of a . . . murder.

Stop thinking that way, she scolded herself. It wasn't a murder. It was an accident. She thought of the body lying there under the crackling, brown leaves. She thought of someone—the dead man's partner—going to the body, tearing the silver skulls from the chain around the dead man's neck. She thought of the plastic ZAP gun lying there beside the body.

Would she really have the nerve to go back to the ravine and retrieve the gun?

Yes. She had no choice. She couldn't leave it there for the police to find.

She thought of the dead man, of his body under the leaves, decaying, decaying, decaying. Would she have to look at him?

No. She'd grab the gun up off the ground and run.

Maybe Pete would come with her. Yes, he probably would.

She looked at Pete, rowing at the front of the canoe, his dark hair blowing in the strong breeze. She realized she was really starting to like him. When she had arrived at the lake an hour before and had seen Gary arrive with Suki, it hadn't bothered her. She had looked at Gary and not felt those pangs, those feelings of "why aren't we together." Now Gary had become just another guy, just another guy from school. And she was glad.

The rain stopped and the cloud cover lightened a bit as they climbed out of the canoes and dragged them onto the rocky beach. The whole island appeared in shades of gray—the trees, the dunes, the beach. Della felt as if she had stepped into a black-and-white movie.

"Pull the canoes over by the trees," Mr. Abner instructed, not noticing that they already were.

We'd better be careful, Della thought. We'd better not give away the fact that we already know the island.

"Is this whole island solid woods?" she asked. "I haven't been here since I was a little girl."

"As far as I know," Mr. Abner said, tugging his canoe with all of the tents and equipment inside. "I've never been to the other side of the island.

Don't know what's over there." He let go of the canoe. "Hey, that's a good idea. Let's hike to the other side of the island. It's a great morning for a hike!"

"Oh no," Suki groaned.

No one else showed much enthusiasm either. "Don't we have to set up the tents and get firewood and stuff first?" Ricky asked hopefully.

"We'll leave everything with the canoes," Mr. Abner said, choosing to ignore their reluctance. "We'll set up when we get back. Come on, everyone. Drop everything and take your backpacks. It won't be a long walk. Just two or three hours at most."

He picked up his blue backpack and swung it onto his shoulders, an excited smile on his face. Della and her friends could see that there was no use grumbling about it. They were going on a hike across the island to the other side.

"Great day for a hike," Pete said, walking next to her, an ironic grin on his face. "How you doing?"

"Me? Okay, I guess. I sure wish this weekend were over." She picked up her backpack. He held it for her while she shoved her arms through the straps.

"You and me both," he said, sighing. The drizzle began again, not exactly rain, but a fine mist that made everything feel wet, even the air they breathed. "I'll go with you to get the ZAP gun. Maybe we can sneak away during the hike."

Della looked up and saw Mr. Abner staring at them. "Maybe we'd better do it after the hike," she whispered.

"We'll go later, when everyone's gathering fire-wood."

"Thanks," she whispered. "I just hope we're not hiking the whole weekend. Mr. Abner is a lot more gung ho about this than I thought he'd be."

They followed the others into the woods. Della pulled up the hood on her sweatshirt. It covered her head and hair, but it didn't keep out the cold or the increasing sense of dread she was feeling. She didn't want to be walking again through these woods, her sneakers crunching over the dead brown leaves.

The ground sloped sharply up. Her sneakers slid on the mud. The footing was getting slippery from the rain. She grabbed Pete's arm and he helped pull her up a steep incline.

They stepped carefully over a fallen tree and followed the others deeper into the woods. Suddenly Mr. Abner came jogging hurriedly back to them, holding a video camera up to his eye. "Don't look at the camera," he instructed, pointing it at Della and Pete, walking backward to keep them in the picture.

They stopped to stare at the camera.

"No—don't stop," he cried. "Keep walking. Act natural."

"Mr. Abner, what are you doing?" Della asked.

"I'm making a complete record of our over-night," he said, still taping them. "When we get back home, I'll make a copy for everyone to keep."

The poor guy, Della thought. He just doesn't know what's going on. He has no idea that this isn't an experience the rest of us are going to want to remember. This camping trip is something we're all going to want to forget as quickly as possible.

"You can at least smile," Mr. Abner urged, walking backward, keeping the video camera fixed on them. Della and Pete made a feeble attempt at smiles. Then, suddenly, Mr. Abner's heel caught on an upraised root and he toppled over backward into the mud.

The six club members tried their best not to laugh. But the sight of him falling onto his backside, video camera leaping out of his hands, his long legs flying into the air, was too hilarious, and they all enjoyed a good laugh. He climbed up slowly, looking embarrassed, and checked over the video camera to make sure it was still functioning.

"Hiking rule number one: Don't face the wrong way when you walk," he said, brushing wet leaves and dirt off the seat of his jeans. Then he added, "I just did that to wake you guys up. That's the first laughter I've heard all morning."

He was right, Della realized. They weren't doing a very good job of acting normal. But what could they do? None of them, not even Ricky, felt like joking around. It was hard for Della to even think straight. She just kept thinking about how she had to sneak away and what she had to do.

They hiked for what seemed like days, stopping only once to eat the sandwiches they had brought. Finally, feeling tired and extremely edgy, they reached their destination. The other side of the island, not surprisingly, looked exactly like the side they knew. The pine trees gave way to the low dunes of a rocky beach. If there was land across this side of the lake, they couldn't see it. Low clouds and fog blocked the view.

"It's kind of pretty," Della said to Pete, staring out at the lake. "So gray and mysterious. It's almost dreamlike."

"I guess," Pete said, shifting his backpack. He groaned. "This thing was light when we started out. Now it weighs a ton."

Mr. Abner finished videotaping the shoreline and lowered his camera. "Doesn't look as if those clouds are going to lift," he said, making a visor with his hand on his forehead to shield his eyes from the glare.

"What do we do now?" Ricky asked him grumpily.

"We head back, of course," Mr. Abner said, still staring across the lake.

"You mean we have to hike back through the woods?" Maia moaned.

"Do you want me to bring the car around?" Mr. Abner asked, laughing. "I'll tell you what, let's go back along the beach. We'll walk around instead of through."

That idea seemed to please everyone. But by the time they made it back to their canoes and supplies, it was late afternoon, their sneakers were soaked, they were chilled through and through, and their legs ached from trudging so far over sand.

Ricky plopped down in one of the canoes. Della and Maia dropped to their knees on the cold, wet, pebbly sand.

"Aah, that was exhilarating!" their advisor cried, smiling happily as he carefully packed away his video camera. "Hey—don't sit down, guys. Fun time is over. Now it's time to start working!"

Muttering and complaining, they carried the tents and supplies to a clearing beyond the tree line. Della realized that they weren't far from their old campsite, a hundred yards or so farther into the trees.

After the tents were put up, Mr. Abner sent them out for firewood. "Try to find dry wood," he instructed.

"Everything's soaking wet," Suki snapped. "Where are we going to find dry wood?"

"I think I have some at home," Ricky offered. "I'll go home for it."

"Ricky—" Mr. Abner said sternly.

"No. Really. I don't mind," Ricky joked. "I'll go get it and be right back."

"Look for wood that's under leaves or under other wood," Mr. Abner said, ignoring Ricky's plea. "It'll be drier than wood that's been exposed. We can burn wood if it's damp. It'll just take a little longer to get going."

The six of them started off in different directions. "Maia, stay here and help me unpack the dinner supplies," Mr. Abner said. Maia immediately turned and headed back into the center of the campsite, looking relieved. "Get lots of wood," their advisor shouted. "Looks like it's going to be a cold, dreary night."

"I don't know about cold, but he's right about dreary," Suki muttered to Gary as they headed off together.

"Bet I can cheer you up," Della heard Gary say to Suki.

"Stop it, Gary. Get your hands off me!" she heard Suki protest, not too convincingly.

Della found Pete tossing wet sticks across the ground. "Nothing is dry," he muttered. "Abner's crazy." A sudden wind came up, shaking tree branches and sending leaves flying in different directions.

"This is the longest day of my life," Della sighed.

"You'll feel better once we . . ." Pete's voice trailed off. He looked around. No one was in sight. "Hey—let's go."

"Huh?"

"Let's go get Ricky's gun. Right now. While there's still a little light."

Della hesitated. She could feel her throat tighten and a heavy feeling begin to grow in her stomach. "I guess . . ."

"Abner's busy with Maia in camp. He won't notice. We'll go grab the gun and be back here in a couple of minutes."

"Okay," Della said, pulling up her sweatshirt hood. "I guess this is as good a time as any."

They started off together in the general direction of the ravine.

"Hey, where are you guys going?" It was Abner.

They turned around, startled to see him in the woods. "We were just, uh—"

"Come on, guys," Abner scolded, shaking his head. "You know the rules. No hanky-panky."

"But we weren't . . ." Della protested.

"Of course you were," Abner insisted, laughing. "Come back closer to camp. You don't have to go this far for wood."

"Okay," Della and Pete said in unison. They

followed him back to the campsite and started gathering firewood at the edge of the tree line.

"We'll never get away. Never," Della moaned.

"Shhh. Look." Pete pointed. Abner and Maia had gone to the other side of the clearing. "Come on. He can't see us. Let's try again."

"Okay. Quick," she said, her eyes on Abner.

"Do you remember exactly where the ravine is?" Pete asked. Her sweatshirt hood was caught in her hair. He helped her straighten it out. His hand felt cold as it brushed against her forehead.

"I . . . I'm pretty sure."

"Then let's go," Pete said.

They hurried into the trees.

As they quickly made their way over the wet, slippery ground, he reached for her hand. He dropped it when they heard the scream.

It came from the campsite, a shrill, ear-piercing scream, a scream of absolute horror.

Della recognized it immediately.

"It's Maia!" she cried.

chapter

14

A second scream tore through the trees, a scream for help.

Della and Pete got to the campsite together, just as Gary and Suki appeared, looking frightened and confused.

"Maia! Where are you?" Della called.

Ricky stumbled into the clearing, carrying a stack of sticks in his hands. He tossed the sticks next to one of the tents. "What's all the racket?"

"Over here!" Maia cried. Her voice came from near the edge of the woods on the other side of the tents. "Help, please!!"

Her heart pounding, Della ran around the tents toward Maia's voice, followed by the others. They found Maia on her knees beside Mr. Abner, who was lying on his back. She was cradling the advisor's head in her arms. As the others drew closer, they could see that his eyes were closed, his mouth open, a rivulet of blood trickling down from his scalp.

"Maia . . . Mr. Abner . . . what . . ."

"He's out cold," Maia told them. "I can't bring him to."

"But who did it?"

"Did you see it happen?"

"Did he fall? Was he . . . shot?"

Pete and Gary knelt down beside Maia. Gary put his hand on Mr. Abner's sweatshirt, above the chest. "His heart is beating okay," he said. "What happened?"

"He was . . . hit," Maia said, her voice trembling. "Hit over the head. I saw someone . . . a man . . . He ran off into the trees." She looked past them to the woods. "That way."

"A man?" Della cried. "Did you get a good look at him?"

"Who was it?" Gary asked.

"I don't know. He was like a blur," Maia said. "A dark blur. He was wearing a black jacket, I think."

Mr. Abner groaned and turned his head, but his eyes didn't open.

"We've got to get help for him," Maia said. She placed his head gently on the ground and backed away. The sleeves of her sweatshirt were stained with dark blood. "He's hurt bad, I think."

Della was surprised at how well Maia reacted in an emergency. She's stronger than anyone gives her credit for, Della thought.

"Who did it? Why?" Suki asked, hands on her hips. She looked more angry than frightened.

"Maybe it's the dead man's partner," Pete said, looking at Della. "Maybe he's followed us back here."

"And now he plans to croak us, one by one," Ricky said, staring into the trees, his round face suddenly tight with fear.

"Shut up, Schorr," Suki snapped. "You always know how to make things worse."

"What could be worse?" Maia said quietly. She ran around to the other side of the tent. A few seconds later she reappeared carrying a rolled-up sleeping bag, which she tucked under Mr. Abner's head. "Someone unfold another sleeping bag and cover him up," she ordered.

Pete ran to get one.

"We're helpless here," Della said, thinking out loud. "We can't help Mr. Abner. And we can't do anything to protect ourselves if—if whoever did it comes back."

"Some of us have got to go to town for help," Maia said, helping Pete spread a sleeping bag over the teacher.

"I'll go!" Ricky cried immediately.

"Not too eager or anything, are you, Schorr?" Suki said.

"Get off my case," Ricky snapped angrily at her.

"Who's gonna make me?" Suki made a face back at him.

"Stop it. Come on, knock it off," Gary said heatedly. "We've got an emergency here."

"He's losing a lot of blood," Maia said, pressing a handkerchief against the side of Mr. Abner's head, trying unsuccessfully to stop the flow.

"Okay. We'll go get help," Gary said. "Come on, Ricky, Suki. Let's go. You three stay and watch him."

Della watched the three of them hurry toward the

canoes. Suddenly, Ricky stopped and turned around. "Hey," he called back, "my ZAP gun. What about my ZAP gun?"

"I'll go get it now," Della answered. She took a deep breath and watched until they disappeared into the trees. "I guess I have no choice," she said to Pete. "I've got to get the gun back. Before they come back with the police."

"Okay. I'll go with you," Pete said, looking down at Mr. Abner. "We'll be back as soon as we can, Maia."

"No!" Maia cried, grabbing his arm. "You can't!"

"What?"

"You can't leave me here alone."

"But Maia—" Della said.

"No. I mean it. That's not fair. What if the man comes back? There won't be anyone here to help me. You can't leave me like that. You just can't."

"She's right," Della told Pete.

"But, Della—"

"I'll have to go get the gun by myself," Della said. "You stay and help Maia."

"But I don't want—"

"We don't want to come back and find Maia hit over the head too. Or worse. It would be our fault, Pete. You've got to stay with her. I'll be right back. I'll run right to the ravine, grab the gun, and run right back."

Pete pulled out of Maia's grasp. "No. I can't let you."

"Look," Della said. She held up the whistle she was wearing around her neck. "See this? I have a whistle. It's real loud. If I'm in any kind of trouble, I'll blow it. Okay?''

"A whistle?" Pete didn't look convinced that this was a good plan. But he looked at Maia, pale and trembling beside him, and realized he had no choice but to let Della go on without him.

"I'll be right back. Really," Della insisted, thinking that maybe if she kept repeating that, she'd start to believe it. She leaned over on tiptoes and gave Pete a quick kiss on the cheek. For luck. Then she turned and forced herself to jog into the woods.

"Wait—stop! Della!" Pete came running after her. "Here. Take this." He handed her a big metal flashlight. "It's getting kind of dark."

She took it from him, surprised by how heavy it was. They turned and walked in opposite directions. She heard Maia calling to him, afraid that he had changed his mind and had left her there.

Maia's such a baby, Della thought.

But then she argued with herself, Maia's right. She has good reason to be scared. And so do I.

She gripped the flashlight tightly. I can use it as a weapon, if I need to, she thought.

A weapon?

What am I thinking of? Have I completely lost my mind? Is this really me, walking through these woods to find a dead man, to retrieve a stupid plastic gun? Alone in the woods while some creep prowls about, some creep who hit Mr. Abner over the head and now might be following me, might be watching me, might be ready to—

Stop!

Just stop thinking, she told herself. Don't think about anything. Keep moving, keep walking till you find the ravine. And shove everything out of your mind. There's nothing you can think about now that will make you feel better. Nothing you can think about that will make you feel any safer.

What about Pete? I'll try thinking about Pete.

But she pictured Pete being hit over the head. Pictured a man in a black jacket running through the trees. Pictured Pete lying on the ground like Mr. Abner, blood trickling down to the ground from his head.

Blood, blood on the ground. Blood everywhere.

No. I can't think about Pete.

I'll think about home. Safe, warm, quiet.

But the dead man's partner was right on my porch, leaving his envelope with the silver skull and the frightening note. Right on my porch. He was practically inside my house. He knows where I live. He knows me. He . . .

Is he watching me now? Is he watching me push my way through the woods? Is he waiting for me to stumble, waiting for me to fall so that he can pounce?

Is he waiting for his revenge, waiting to pay me back for killing his friend, for burying his friend in leaves and running away?

No!

Stop thinking!

Della looked around and realized she had lost her sense of direction. It all looked the same to her, the rustling trees, the clumps of brown weeds, the floating, shifting dead leaves.

Had she been here before? Was she walking in circles?

No. This had to be the right direction. She remembered that large, square rock at the bottom of the low hill.

Yes. She was heading to the ravine. She was nearly there. Maybe.

She just had to concentrate on where she was going, chase these other thoughts from her head.

It suddenly grew darker, as if someone had turned off some lights. She clicked on the flashlight, throwing a narrow beam of white light on the ground ahead of her.

Yes. That was better. At least she could see the ground now, could see to step over that fallen branch and step around that hole and walk away from those clumps of thorns.

It's right up here, I think. She stared over the beam of light, trying to see through the trees. She was climbing a steep slope now. Yes. She remembered it. She remembered how steep it suddenly became, how surprisingly steep and—

What was that light?

To her right she saw a flash of white light through the trees.

Was that just my light? A reflection of my light?

No. She saw it again, a narrow beam, cut off by a branch.

Thinking quickly, she clicked off her flashlight. Why give away where I am?

A chill went down her back. She struggled to catch her breath.

Who was it?

The light disappeared, then reappeared a few feet away, a few feet closer. The light seemed to flicker and float, as if free of gravity, as if emitted by some giant firefly hovering among the trees.

Maybe it's Pete.

Yes, of course. It's Pete. He got Maia settled down and came after me.

Should she call to him?

Yes. No. Yes. But what if it isn't Pete? What if it's the creep who hit Mr. Abner?

No. Don't call to him.

The light moved closer.

"Pete?" Her voice came out tiny and frightened. The word just slipped out. She hadn't meant to say it. But now that she had, she repeated it. "Pete?" A little louder this time.

The light floated closer. She could hear footsteps now.

"Pete?"

A cough. She heard a man's cough.

It wasn't Pete.

He was coming toward her now.

She froze. How stupid. How stupid to call out and let him know where she was. To bring him right to her.

No! Stop thinking! Stop thinking—and run.

She turned and started to flee. She wasn't think- ing about anything now. Her mind was empty, clear. All thoughts had been chased away by her fear.

She was just running, listening to the crunch of fast-approaching footsteps behind her, and running, running over the slippery, brown leaves, over the fallen limbs and branches, through burrs and bram- bles and clumps of tall, stringy weeds.

She gripped the flashlight tightly in her hand, but she hadn't turned it on. She hadn't time. And she didn't need it. She was running on radar now, the radar of fear. It carried her through the darkness.

But the light behind her was floating closer, closer.

She was climbing now, up a steep slope, climbing away from the light, toward—

Before she realized it, she was near the top of the incline. Before she realized it, she was at its crest. Then over it. She didn't stop, didn't see the fallen tree in her path.

She stumbled, didn't cry out, didn't make a sound, too frightened to scream. She knew where she was. She knew where she was falling.

She knew she had found the ravine. And as she fell forward, almost diving down the side, she saw the dreadful, dreadful pile of leaves—and knew she was falling right onto it.

chapter
15

*S*he was right on top of him.

I'm going to be sick, she thought. A wave of nausea rolled up from her stomach. She took a deep breath and held it, waiting for the feeling to pass.

Dizzy. I'm so dizzy.

She tried to push herself up with her arms, but her hands slipped on the wet leaves.

I'm right on top of him, on top of his dead, decaying body.

She forced herself to her feet, still holding her breath, still feeling dizzy.

I was lying on top of a dead man.

The flashlight. Where was the flashlight?

That's it, Della. Think about the flashlight. Think about finding the ZAP gun and getting out of this ravine. Don't think about the leaf pile. Don't think about the decaying, rotting body you were just lying on. Don't think—

Wait. The leaf pile. It was so flat. She remembered the mound of leaves they had left there.

Well . . . maybe a lot of the leaves had blown away.

Gingerly, she kicked at the leaves with her sneaker.

They fell away at her touch.

She kicked again, probing deeper into the pile.

Nothing but leaves.

Breathing heavily, she stepped onto the leaf pile. Her sneaker sank down deep until it touched . . .

. . . the ground!

She kicked at the leaves, again, again, sending them flying in all directions.

He was gone. The body was gone. He wasn't in the leaf pile.

The body had been moved.

She stood staring at the scattered leaves. She didn't know how to feel. She felt relieved that she hadn't been lying on top of the decaying body. But the fact that he'd been moved brought a flood of questions to her mind.

Shaking her head as if that could clear it, she bent down low and searched in the leaves for the ZAP gun. She shoved the leaves aside with both hands, pawing at them like a dog trying to dig up a lost bone.

Not finding the gun, she stood up and began plowing through the whole area, dragging her sneaker slowly in straight lines, kicking into clumps of matted leaves.

No success.

"I've got to find it," she said aloud. "I've got to."

She dragged her shoe across a wider area, with no success. "It's *got* to be here," she muttered to herself, bending low and scrabbling among the leaves.

Her hand hit something hard.

Startled, she picked it up. It was her flashlight.

This should be a help, she thought. She clicked it on. No light. She clicked it again. Again.

It must have broken during her fall.

Frustrated, she banged it against the side of her jeans leg.

"Ouch!"

Take it easy, girl. Don't lose control.

The light still wouldn't come on.

She was about to toss the flashlight away when she heard the cough.

Behind her.

She spun around.

Someone was standing above her in the darkness. First she saw his black, mud-splattered boots. Then she saw his straight-legged jeans.

Her eyes went up to the leather bomber jacket.

"NO! IT CAN'T BE!" she screamed in a voice she didn't recognize. "YOU WERE DEAD! I KNOW YOU WERE DEAD!"

With a growl more animal than human, he leaped off the side of the ravine, hurtling himself at her and grabbing her throat with both hands.

chapter
16

*D*ella dropped backward, slipping away from him.

Breathing loudly, growling with each breath, he took a step back and lunged at her again.

Without thinking, without realizing she was even doing it, she raised her arm. And when he came near enough, she brought the flashlight down on his head as hard as she could.

It made a loud *thud*. Metal against bone.

The flashlight came on, sending a white beam of light to the ground.

She suddenly felt as if someone else had done it. Someone else's arm had swung down. Someone else's hand had gripped the flashlight. Someone else had cracked it over the man's skull.

But her fear was real. She could taste it now.

Fear tastes bitter, she realized.

She dropped down to her knees in the leaves. Everything was spinning about her, the trees, the ground beneath her, the man lying so still at her side. Spinning, spinning. If only she could get the bitter taste out of her mouth . . .

She waited, keeping her head low, taking deep breaths. She waited for the spinning to stop, waited for her heartbeats to slow.

After a while she began to feel better. She climbed back to her feet. She raised the flashlight and shined it into the unconscious man's face.

"Ohh!" She stared at the face, so pale in the white beam of light, at the closed eyes, at the curly blond hair, at the short, upturned nose, at the long, straight scar across the chin.

It wasn't the same man.

It wasn't the dead man, the man she had shoved down the ravine during the first overnight.

She kept the light on his face until her hand began to shake so badly she couldn't keep the beam steady. Then she turned away from him to think.

This must be the partner, she realized.

Of course. Of course this is the partner.

And then she thought, I just want to get away from here

She no longer cared about Ricky's ZAP gun, about where the dead man's body had been moved, about the partner, about *anything*. She just wanted to run away, run back to camp, to get Pete and Maia and paddle away from Fear Island and all of its terrors—forever.

Without looking back at the man on the ground, she aimed the light ahead of her, up the steep, muddy side of the ravine, and began to climb. It was too slippery to walk up, so she used her hands too, climbing like an animal, struggling to keep hold of the flashlight as she pulled herself up to the top.

When she made it to the top, the knees of her jeans were soaked through with mud. They felt cold and wet against her legs as she started to run back toward the campsite, keeping the beam of light low in front of her. Her hands were raw and caked with wet mud.

Branches slapped at her face as she ran. A large thorn ripped a long tear in her sweatshirt. She cried out, more in surprise than in pain, but didn't slow her pace.

"I've got to get back, got to get back," she said aloud, the words coming between gasps for air.

The others were probably back from town by now. And they'd have brought the police or a doctor or someone.

Not far to go. Not far to go and she'd be safe.

"Ohhh!"

She fell headfirst over a fallen tree limb.

"I'm okay. I'm okay. Got to keep going."

She pulled herself up quickly. Her left hand was cut. She could feel the warm blood trickling down her wrist.

Got to keep going.

The trees thinned out. She was almost there.

Then she heard the footsteps behind her.

The partner?

No. He couldn't have followed her that easily, couldn't have caught up to her that fast.

It must be Pete, she realized.

As soon as the others got back from town, Pete must have set out to look for her.

Slowing to a stop, she reached for the whistle around her neck, brought it to her lips and blew it.

No sound came out. She shook it. The whistle had no little ball inside.

"Great protection," she sighed, and dropped the whistle disgustedly.

"Pete!" she cried out. "Pete! Over here! I'm okay, Pete! I'm over here!"

She ran toward the sound of his steps.

A foot kicked out from behind a tree, and she tripped over it, crying out in surprise as she landed on her hands and knees in soft mud.

A laugh.

She turned quickly and looked up at him.

The dead man. The man she had killed.

"You're dead," she blurted out, staying down on the ground, staring up into his angry, dark eyes. "You're dead. I know you're dead."

"Okay. I'm a ghost," he said quietly. He shrugged and stepped out from behind the tree. He was wearing the same leather bomber jacket.

"But . . . no! You had no pulse. I checked it. Gary—he checked it too."

The young man stood over her, his handsome face twisted in a sneer, his hands poised in case she tried to move away. "I'm a medical freak," he said softly, calmly. "No lie. I have a very faint pulse point. Even doctors have trouble finding it."

"Really?" she asked weakly. She glanced quickly to either side, trying to figure out the best escape route.

"So it was you all along," she said. "But why? Why were you trying to scare us? Just for revenge?"

"Revenge?" He laughed, a dry, bitter laugh. "What a stupid word."

"Then why?" she repeated.

He shrugged. "We didn't get anything from the old gardener. Not a dime. If he had money hidden away, we sure didn't find it. That was very disappointing. So when you came along and did your little burial number on me, we got an idea. First, we wanted to scare you a bit. You know, soften you up, make it easier to squeeze a little money from you and your kind parents. How much would *you* have been willing to pay to keep things quiet about the murder—my murder?"

He kicked the trunk of a tree, unable to hold in his anger. "Your parents have a lot of dough. They'd probably part with some of it . . . to keep it quiet that their daughter was a murderer."

"But I wasn't!" Della protested. "You weren't dead."

"Details." He grinned.

"Was that you in the black Taurus, out on Old Mill Road?" she asked.

"That was my buddy." He chuckled. "Just having some fun. But I guess you gave him more fun than he bargained for. Poor guy had to walk back through the woods."

"So the skulls . . . the note . . . all to scare us so we'd pay you?"

He grinned. "I guess you could say that. Yeah. We wanted to have a little fun first. Then get down to business."

They stared at each other. Della had spotted a clear path through the trees. If she could only catch him off balance for a second, she figured, she could make a run for it.

As if reading her thoughts, he grabbed her. "You

stupid fool," he said, pulling his face close to hers. "Why didn't you check to see if I was breathing?"

"Ow. My arm! You're hurting me!"

He tightened his grip instead of loosening it.

"Why?" he demanded. "Why didn't you check to see if I was breathing?"

"I—I was scared," she said, trying to pull away from his grasp, trying to pull away from the pain. "I was too scared. I just couldn't—I couldn't think clearly. Everything was spinning around. I couldn't figure out *what* to do."

"That's not true!" he screamed in her face, his eyes wild and crazy. He loosened his grip on her arms just a little. "You didn't care," he sneered. "You didn't care enough to see if I was breathing or not!"

"No!" she protested.

"Shut up!" He let go of one arm, brought his hand back and slapped her face hard with the back of his hand.

"No!"

"Shut up! Shut up! Shut up!" He was in a rage.

She stood still, looking down at the ground, her cheek throbbing with pain, and waited for him to calm down. He still gripped one arm, his face close to hers, his hot breath on her face.

Finally he let go and took a step back.

"I'm not a bad guy, really. Some girls say I'm pretty good-looking. What do *you* say?"

His rage had cooled. He was playing with her now, teasing her, testing her.

She didn't want to say or do anything to make him explode again with anger. But what was the right answer?

If only she could break free, she was sure she could run away. The campsite couldn't be far. But right now it seemed as if it were on the other side of the world!

"Well?" He was waiting for an answer.

"Yes. Yes, you're good-looking," she said, looking away from him, trying to avoid his eyes, which were burning into hers. "Very good-looking."

"Say it sincere," he said.

"What?"

"You heard me!" he screamed. "Say it sincere!"

"I *was* sincere," she said weakly, seeing his temper flare.

"Well, maybe this will help you feel a little more sincere." He reached into his pocket, then held something up in front of her face.

It was a pistol.

"No!" she screamed. She hadn't meant to scream, but in that instant she realized that he meant to kill her.

Her fear made her act. She jerked away from him, started to run.

But he caught her quickly, grabbed her arm and spun her around.

His dark eyes were wild with fury. "No!" he screamed. "No! No! No! You're supposed to be *friendly!* Don't you know *anything?*"

He raised the pistol and pressed its barrel against her temple.

"No, please . . ." she managed to say, her voice a whisper.

"You had your chance!" he screamed.

He pulled the trigger.

chapter

17

She didn't have time to scream.

First, she realized she was still alive. Then, she felt the stream of liquid trickling down the side of her face.

Paint. He had shot her with the ZAP gun.

She reached up and rubbed her fingers in it just to make sure. Yes. Yellow paint.

He let go of her and began laughing, pointing and shaking his head, finding her fear, the frozen look of horror on her face, hilarious. He laughed louder, harder, closing his eyes, pointing, the cruelest laugh she'd ever heard.

He twirled the ZAP gun on his finger and shot a stream of paint into the air. This made him laugh even harder. He had tears in his eyes. His laugh became high-pitched. He was laughing so hard, he had to gasp for breath.

This is it, Della thought. This is my chance.

She turned and started to run. She had already picked the route for her escape. His laughter was the distraction she needed to try it. She knew she would have only a few seconds' head start—but maybe, just maybe, a few seconds would be all she needed.

She moved quickly, almost floating over the ground. As she ran, the sudden freedom made her feel light. She had the surprising feeling that if she wanted to, she could fly.

Fly away, Della. Fly away.

I've never run this fast, she thought.

She was startled when he tackled her around the waist and brought her crashing to the ground.

Landing hard on her side, she groaned in pain as he fell on top of her. It felt as if she'd cracked a rib.

He got up slowly, looking down at her, all of the mirth gone from his face. It was as if the laughter had never existed. Now his face revealed only anger.

He pulled her up roughly and gave her a hard shove backward. "You shouldn't have done that," he said, breathing heavily. He shook his head. "No, you shouldn't have tried that."

He looked down at the ZAP gun. He had dropped it before tackling her. She held her aching side. The pain was starting to fade. Probably nothing broken.

"I've got a real gun too," he said softly. "I used it on that old guy in the house. I can use it again."

"No," Della said, wiping wet dirt off her hands. She didn't see any real gun. But she wasn't about to challenge him.

"I can use it again," he repeated, his eyes growing wild as his anger rose. "I don't have any problem with it, really. If that's what it takes to communicate. I only want to communicate, you know. It shouldn't be so hard. People to people. That kind of deal. You know what I mean? So why should it be so hard? Why should it be so hard for people to understand? Why should I have to use a gun? You know where I'm coming from, don't you? You look like a smart girl. You see what I mean, don't you?"

He stopped, as if waiting for an answer.

She stared back at him. She didn't know what to say. "Yes, I see," she said finally.

He's crazy, she realized. He's totally off-the-wall.

She suddenly felt like screaming.

I'm trapped here with a total crazy person. He could do anything to me. *Anything!*

"What are you going to do to me?" she blurted out.

He blinked, surprised by the interruption. His angry expression faded, replaced by a blank stare. "What does it matter?" he asked bitterly. "I'm dead anyway, right?"

"No," she stuttered.

His anger flooded back. He grabbed her arm. "I'm dead anyway, right? You buried me under a pile of leaves, remember? I'm not even here—right?"

"No! I mean—"

"I'm dead. I'm a dead man, a dead man," he repeated, pulling her close.

"No! Please!"

The bright light startled Della almost as much as it did her captor.

There were moving shadows, the crunch of footsteps, and then a triangle of bright, white light.

The light beamed into the young man's eyes. He made a face and let go of Della. "Hey—I can't see!" He raised his hands to shield his eyes.

Another hand pulled at Della's arm. "Come on—let's go!"

"Pete!" she cried, everything coming into focus at last.

Pete was shining his bright halogen lantern into the man's eyes. "Come on!" he cried.

But Della didn't follow immediately. Thinking quickly, she bent down and picked up the ZAP gun. The man lowered his hands to see what was happening. And she fired twice, three times, four.

He cried out. The paint burned his eyes. He covered them again, screaming blindly in pain.

It was time to run.

"No—this way!" Pete yelled.

She had been heading in the wrong direction all along.

She turned and followed him, stumbling over a low tree stump.

"Hurry, Della! He's coming after us!"

Della turned, saw him running after them, still rubbing his eyes. Did he have a gun, as he had boasted? If he did, she knew he'd use it. He had certainly made that clear to her.

She pulled herself up and started running again. "Pete—don't wait for me! Just run!" she called.

But Pete waited for her to catch up. "It took me so long to find you. I'm not going back without you!" he cried.

They ran together, side by side, each looking

back every few seconds. Their pursuer was still chasing them. He was no longer rubbing his eyes. But he was running uncertainly, carefully, as if he couldn't really see where he was going.

"Almost there," Pete cried, breathing hard.

"I . . . I can't . . ." she moaned. "I can't . . . go any farther. I . . ."

He grabbed her hand. "Come on. You can make it."

They looked back. The man in the bomber jacket was gaining on them. "Come back! I want to talk to you!" he screamed at the top of his lungs.

The sound of his voice, so loud, so close, so out of control, made them run even faster.

"Stop! I just want to talk! That's all—really! Stop! I just want to *communicate* with you!"

Della's side ached and she felt she couldn't breathe, but she kept pace with Pete. Finally they reached the clearing, and seeing the tents and her friends and the small campfire, she leaped forward, lunged with her whole body. She was flying now, floating above the ground, above the pain, because she was back in camp and safe.

Gasping for breath, she dropped to her knees in front of the fire. Maia and Suki came running over to help her, to comfort her.

And the young man in the bomber jacket stepped into the clearing.

"There he is!" she heard Pete yell.

She heard running feet. There was a lot of movement, a lot of confusion.

She looked up, startled to see three policemen burst into the campsite. At first Della thought it was a dream, a hallucination brought on by her long run, her exhaustion, her fear.

But the policemen were real.

The young man stared at them in disbelief. He didn't move, made no attempt to escape.

They circled him and grabbed him easily. He didn't even try to resist. He was too surprised, too winded, too weary to fight back. "Where'd *you* come from?" he asked, looking very bewildered.

"Cincinnati," a red-faced young policeman cracked. "Where'd *you* come from?"

"Mars," was the bitter reply.

"I don't care where he came from," another policeman said, giving him a hard shove. "But I know where he's going."

"You cops know everything," the man in the bomber jacket said under his breath.

"Read him his rights," the third policeman said. Then he hurried over to Della. "You okay, miss?"

"Yeah. I guess," Della said uncertainly. "He was holding me in the woods. He wanted to—"

"That's okay." The policeman put a hot, heavy hand on her shoulder. "You can tell us about it later. Take a little while to catch your breath." He started back to the others.

"His partner—" Della started.

The policeman turned quickly, very interested. "Yeah?"

"His partner's in the woods. In the ravine. I'll take you there."

"Okay. Let me radio the station first." He called to his two buddies. "Hey . . . the partner's here too. In the woods!" Then he turned back to Della. "You know, there's a reward for these two guys."

Della smiled at Pete, who was pouring a canteen of water over his head, trying to cool down. He smiled back at her through the water trickling down his face.

"The best reward," she said, "is that this nightmare is over."

chapter

18

"W here are you going tonight?" Della's mother asked, straightening Della's hair with her hand.

Della pulled away. Her mother was always rearranging her hair after she'd gotten it just the way she wanted it. "To a movie, I guess. Or maybe to Pete's house to watch some tapes. Pete didn't really say."

"Well, a movie's okay," her mother said, straightening a sofa cushion. "I don't want you staying out too late." Her mother stared at her from across the room, a thoughtful look on her face.

She's probably thinking about all the horrible things I told her, Della thought. After confessing to their parents—and the police—all that had happened since their first unchaperoned overnight, it was hard for any of them to think about anything else.

Della had spent most of the week thinking about it all, reliving it, even dreaming about it at night.

Now, a week later, it was time to shove it out of her mind, go out, have a great Saturday night.

The doorbell rang and she hurried to answer it. "Hi, Pete."

"How's it going, Della?"

"Great." She called good-night to her mother, stepped out, and closed the front door behind them.

A few minutes later, they were heading toward town in his family's station wagon. "Hey—wait a minute!" Della cried, alarmed. "What's *that?*"

She was pointing to the folded-up green tent in the back of the car.

"Oh, that," Pete said, grinning. "I thought you might like to go camping out!"

She slugged him on the shoulder as hard as she could.

"Just a joke! Just a joke!" he protested, cowering, trying to edge away from any other punches. "I'm taking that in to be patched for my brother's scout troop."

"Well, okay," she said, laughing and settling back in the seat. "From now on, the only camping I want to do is in front of the TV set in the den!"

"That sounds good to me too," Pete said, motioning for her to move closer to him on the seat. "But can you roast marshmallows in front of the TV?"

"We can try," Della said, moving close. "We can try."

ABOUT THE AUTHOR

R. L. STINE is the author of more than 70 books of humor, adventure and mystery for young readers. In recent years, he has been concentrating on scary thrillers such as this one.

For ten years he was the editor of *Bananas*, a national humor magazine for young people. In addition to magazine and book writing, he is currently Head Writer of the children's TV show "Eureeka's Castle."

He lives in New York City with his wife Jane and son Matthew.

THE NIGHTMARES
NEVER END . . .
WHEN YOU VISIT
FEAR STREET

NEXT: *MISSING*

Mark and Cara's parents are missing.
And no one in town—not even the police—
will help find them. Why have they disappeared?
The mysterious boarder up in the attic has some of
the answers, as does Mark's terrified girlfriend.
The trail of clues leads Mark and Cara to a weird
secret cult—and to murder. And they realize
someone wants *them* to become missing too!

FEAR STREET

R.L. Stine

- ☐ THE NEW GIRL.............74649-9/$3.90
- ☐ THE SURPRISE PARTY.....73561-6/$3.99
- ☐ THE OVERNIGHT............74650-9/$3.99
- ☐ MISSING......................69410-3/$3.99
- ☐ THE WRONG NUMBER......69411-1/$3.99
- ☐ THE SLEEPWALKER.........74652-9/$3.99
- ☐ HAUNTED....................74651-0/$3.99
- ☐ HALLOWEEN PARTY.........70243-2/$3.99
- ☐ THE STEPSISTER............70244-0/$3.99
- ☐ SKI WEEKEND...............72480-0/$3.99
- ☐ THE FIRE GAME.............72481-9/$3.99
- ☐ THE THRILL CLUB...........78581-8/$3.99
- ☐ LIGHTS OUT.................72482-7/$3.99
- ☐ TRUTH or DARE.............86836-5/$3.99

- ☐ THE SECRET BEDROOM.....72483-5/$3.99
- ☐ THE KNIFE...................72484-3/$3.99
- ☐ THE PROM QUEEN...........72485-1/$3.99
- ☐ FIRST DATE.................73865-8/$3.99
- ☐ THE BEST FRIEND...........73866-6/$3.99
- ☐ THE CHEATER...............73867-4/$3.99
- ☐ SUNBURN....................73868-2/$3.99
- ☐ THE NEW BOY...............73869-0/$3.99
- ☐ THE DARE...................73870-4/$3.99
- ☐ BAD DREAMS................78569-9/$3.99
- ☐ DOUBLE DATE...............78570-2/$3.99
- ☐ ONE EVIL SUMMER..........78596-6/$3.99
- ☐ THE MIND READER..........78600-8/$3.99
- ☐ WRONG NUMBER 2..........8607-5/$3.99
- ☐ DEAD END ....86837-3/$3.99
- ☐ FINAL GRADE...............86838-1/$3.99
- ☐ SWITCHED..................86839-X/$3.99

FEAR STREET SAGA

- ☐ #1: THE BETRAYAL.... 86831-4/$3.99
- ☐ #2: THE SECRET.......86832-2/$3.99
- ☐ #3: THE BURNING.......86833-0/$3.99

SUPER CHILLER

- ☐ PARTY SUMMER......72920-9/$3.99
- ☐ BROKEN HEARTS.....78609-1/$3.99
- ☐ THE DEAD LIFEGUARD ....86834-9/$3.99

CHEERLEADERS

- ☐ THE FIRST EVIL..........75117-4/$3.99
- ☐ THE SECOND EVIL....75118-2/$3.99
- ☐ THE THIRD EVIL.......75119-0/$3.99
- ☐ THE NEW EVIL..............86835-7/$3.99

99 FEAR STREET: THE HOUSE OF EVIL

- ☐ THE FIRST HORROR ....88562-6/$3.99
- ☐ THE SECOND HORROR........88563-4 /$3.99
- ☐ THE THIRD HORROR.............88564-2/$3.99

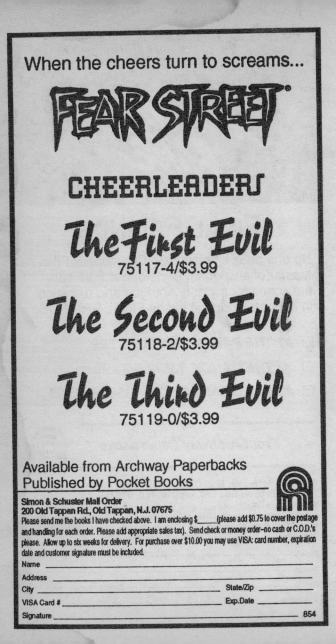